Brawn or Bust

Pook laid a heavy glamour on the two of us. Under the glamour, my hair got redder and longer, my muscles filled out—becoming corded and knotted with real troll mass—and I put on at least ten stone in weight.

Pook—well, he got muscle and lost tail.

We looked older and bigger and much more knowing than we really were.

We looked swell.

In our grown-up troll disguises, we climbed the hill. The road crew were already out of the trucks and looking over the site. They all wore dark Levi's and black tour T-shirts with yellow lettering:

BOOTS AND THE
SEVEN LEAGUERS
Pay the Troll

"Hey!" I called out, startled at how deep my voice suddenly sounded. "Need some help?"

One of the drivers laughed. "Roadies? Why not! We could use the extra hands. Work all day, and we'll give you comps for the show."

And just like that

Boots and the Seven Leaguers: A Rock-and-Troll Novel

Jane Yolen
AR B.L.: 4.2
Points: 4.0   MG

Boots and the
Seven Leaguers

Boots and the Seven Leaguers

A Rock-and-Troll Novel

Jane Yolen

Magic Carpet Books
Harcourt, Inc.
ORLANDO   AUSTIN   NEW YORK   SAN DIEGO   TORONTO   LONDON

www.HarcourtBooks.com

First Magic Carpet Books edition 2003

Magic Carpet Books is a trademark of Harcourt, Inc., registered in
the United States of America and/or other jurisdictions.

The Library of Congress has cataloged the hardcover edition as follows:
Yolen, Jane.
Boots and the Seven Leaguers:
a rock-and-troll novel/Jane Yolen.
p. cm.
Summary: Teen troll Gog and his best friend Pook work as roadies
for a troll rock and roll band until Gog's younger brother
gets kidnapped.
[1. Trolls—Fiction. 2. Kidnapping—Fiction.] I. Title.
PZ7.Y78Bm 2000
[Fic]—dc21 00-8594
ISBN 0-15-202557-X
ISBN 0-15-202563-4 pb

Text set in Granjon
Display type set in Alcoholica
Designed by Lori McThomas Buley

A C E G H F D B

To Adam, Betsy, and the Boo (a.k.a. Alison)—
Rock and roll!
And to Michael Stearns, who loved it first.

TABLE OF CONTENTS

Boots and the
Seven Leaguers

Meet me under the bridge tonight.
We're going to pick up a friend
Or pick a fight.
Tonight.

— "Meet Me," from BRIDGE BOUND

CHAPTER ONE

SIGNS

There were signs all over the Kingdom, all over Erl-king Hollow.

Not the usual signs, the ones full of magic and the haze of glamour.

These signs were posters announcing that Boots and the Seven Leaguers, the greatest rock-and-troll band in the world, were coming to play Rhymer's Bridge in three days.

On the full moon.

Three days—and me without a ticket!

No ticket...and no coins to buy one. I'd spent all my pocket money on a box of magic cards. But the only magic they'd produced was a lightening of my pockets.

However, I *had* managed to scam one of the band's new posters for my room. A super-realistic, gnarly, snarly full-color shot of the band.

I'd grabbed it from an alley wall near the hind end of the City, a place where I knew that no one would stop me from taking it. (Not like they would in the center of the City, where I'd have been reported to the Queen's Men and hauled off to the Doom Room for questioning. The Queen's Men rule the Kingdom with a heavy hand.)

That alley had been dark and scary, a gathering place for old posters and older spells. A phosphorescent green slime drizzled down the wall. Broken bottles littered the cracked pavement. There was a smell there I couldn't quite catch.

All the kids in the Kingdom know about that alley. It's a place of wild magic. The kind no one controls. Yeah—we all know about that alley. But few are foolish enough to go in there.

Not unless they're desperate.

Desperation and magic—that's a dangerous combination. It has killed some of the Folk, and many humans. But we trolls come in a large size and are made of stronger stuff. So I went in.

Just grab the poster and run, I reminded myself, though I have to admit my back was wet with the sweating fears.

I swear daylight hadn't shone in that alley in years. Centuries, even.

The bones of what-I-dared-not-name lay scattered in the dust. Maybe they belonged to the elf who'd put the poster there in the first place. I could just make out the bones in the shadows, a jumble of white, like the remains of somebody's dinner.

It's not true that nothing frightens a troll.

Dead folk give me the heebie-jeebies.

But I wanted that poster and I was determined to get it.

Besides, I figured that whoever was dead in the alley wouldn't be going to the concert anyway, so what did he need the poster for? But just in case, I went in quick to strip the poster from the wall.

Strip—and get out of there.

The poster was stuck tighter than a ghoul's sucker, and I had to slow down or rip it.

Behind me I could hear those bones starting to re-assemble themselves, the *clickety-clack* of tibias and fibulas and who-knows-what-else clattering together. And a hint of dark, uncontrolled magic collecting behind the bones, giving them a push.

Whoever lay there wasn't just dead.

He was undead.

Bad cess—even for trolls.

I worked my thumbnail under the poster and then up along the side.

Click.

Clack.

I could hear the bones nestling together, but I had half the poster off the wall and didn't want to stop.

Clickety-clack.

And then I had it off entirely. What was underneath stopped me for a moment. It was a picture of a missing pixie child, his pointed ears drooping. He'd been squinting into the camera. But that was none of my lookout. Trolls don't mix with pixies.

Clickety-clickety-clack.

I turned and—rolling the poster up as I ran—made for the light, moving faster than my mother would have thought possible.

Of course, I didn't look back. I knew better than that. If I were to see the assembled bones over my left shoulder, the bones could follow me all night.

Clickety-clickety-clack-clack.

If I saw them over my right, I'd be following him. That's the way bone magic works in the hind end of the City.

Everybody knows that.

Mr. Standing Bones clearly considered that poster his own. I could hear him as he started after me.

Click.

Clack.

Never, I thought. I'd never go back into that alley again. Not for anything. Not even for Boots and the band. Though I didn't drop the poster.

My mouth was dry and I grabbed my breath in gulps. I ran back into the sun, where the dark couldn't gather.

Suddenly the clicks and clacks stopped.

I didn't turn, but I could guess. The skeleton couldn't chase me out into the sun, the undead being shadow folk. And while trolls aren't great fans of the sun—we go grey as ash, grey as stone, under its light—this was one time that I welcomed its warmth on my face.

Still, the sticky hand of horror lay across my back long after I hit the bright street, so I kept running another block to be sure, and ran right into the center of the City.

I stopped by the entrance to the Queen's winter palace, unrolled the poster, and grinned.

By the Law of Finders, the poster was now mine—and it was awesome. Gnarly, snarly, indeed.

The band members were wearing all leather, with hard knobs and studded wristers, and tight leather trews. Boots had a bloodred bandanna around his black dreads and six new gold rings in his ears. Armstrong was snarling out at the camera, one hand holding her bodhran and the other clutched around a bottle of Dregs. Cal and Iggy were pretending to bite the heads off of chickens, and maybe Cal was pretending a bit too much because blood was trickling down his chin and the chicken looked really unhappy.

Which is cool.

And as usual, Booger was way off to the side of the picture looking bored.

It was the greatest poster I'd ever seen, and it was going right over my bed, whether Mom complained or not.

It's my room, after all.

Well—my *half* of the room.

The other half belongs to my baby brother, Magog, who is small for his age and light for a troll and wears glasses made by a boggle, so who cares what Magog thinks. Except, Magog likes the band as much as I do.

The band comes through the Kingdom only once a year these days. Mostly they play for humans out in the Out, not for us Folk in the In. They've won a Grammy and a platinum record and they're so big outside the Kingdom that they don't need to play for the Fey anymore, except that they aren't so big that they've forgotten their roots. Here. In the Kingdom.

After all, Boots was born just upriver from me, under Netherstone Bridge, which makes him kind of kin. Bridge trolls hang together, of course. The other band members are all Middle Kingdom trolls, which makes them kin as well. We trolls hold on to our kinship lines as a sacred trust. We may fight among ourselves—but don't you try and fight against any one of us. Then you'll have the whole lot of us to contend with.

Some of the kids say Boots and the band play the

Kingdom just because they *have* to come here once a year or they'll never get back In again. That staying away for an entire run of the sun locks you out of the Kingdom forever. And then they'd be Out there with humans instead of In here with us Fey. Humans may have electricity, but they've got no power. My best friend, Pook, told me he read that in *The Rules of the Kingdom.*

But I didn't believe him. He's a pookah and as they are all tricksters and shape-changers, you can't always trust them. Even when one's your best friend.

I knew better anyway. The band was playing here because no matter how famous they get in the Out— the outside world—what's really important to them is what's In. *In* the Kingdom. Boots said so in an interview in *People,* though not in the cover story. I found the magazine floating near one of the Kingdom's doors. It wasn't so soaked I couldn't dry it out and read it.

There it was in print. "I'll always be loyal to the Kingdom," Boots said.

So it *has* to be true.

And now they were going to do a one-nighter at Rhymer, just like they say on *Bridge Bound,* their first album. You know:

> *First timer,*
> *Under Rhymer,*
> *Where cooler waters flow.*

That makes me real proud—bridges both over and under being important to us trolls, and Rhymer's Bridge being the most important bridge in the Kingdom.

Boots and the Seven Leaguers playing under the bridge made me feel close and connected to the whole band. Almost as if I were one of them.

So I knew that somehow I was going to have to get to see them.

I just *had* to.

Even if I didn't have a ticket.

Or the coins to buy one.

Yet.

You can always get something from a greenman,
But you might not like what you get.

— "Greenman," from BRIDGE BOUND

CHAPTER TWO

GREENMAN

If I couldn't get a ticket anywhere else, I knew I could always go to a greenman.

Of course, Mom had warned me and warned me against them. Don't all mothers?

"Trolls," she always says, "are an ancient race. Blah-de-blah." (Insert your ancestry lines here. Mom always does.)

"And we never had to hang around the greenmen in the olden days." (Read *really* ancient times.)

"And you shouldn't be tempted to now, Gog. They're just a bad lot." (It's the same old stuff. I stop listening almost immediately. I mean, how often can you hear about temptation, the whys and wherefores, and not want to throw up?)

When I was young and hairless and bridge-bound, having to stay close to my own bridge when not in the company of a grown-up, I wasn't tempted by the greenmen. Not even a little. So I guess I get no awards for the straight line there.

Of course, once I had hair down past my shoulders and was old enough to go up- and downstream on my own, there was always a greenkid or two or three sitting on the riverbank, with their cool camo outfits and hawk feathers laced into their dark braids. They like to laze around and call out to anyone passing by, "Wanna try some...?" Offering up grasses of all kinds: dried rye and timothy and golden alfalfa from the Forbidden Fields.

And of course *they* always have tickets to whatever is coming through the Kingdom. I don't know how, but they do.

Sure, we all know they're a bad lot—not just tricksy like the pookahs, who might get you into trouble but would never try to hurt you. You don't ever trust pookahs, even though you can live with them. But it's the very badness of the Greenman and his kin that is so...well...tempting.

So, even if I didn't actually hang *with* them, I hung *near* them. Dangerous but deliciously near.

All the kids in the Kingdom do it. It's called *banking:* when you climb up on the riverbank as close to a greenkid as you dare.

But not too close, of course.

Pook told me he once banked so close to the Greenman himself—that ageless rogue—that he could count the green nose hairs.

Not that I believed Pook entirely. I mean, I didn't even know if the Greenman *has* nose hairs. Or if they are green.

But I sure don't tell my mom about banking. If I told her that, I'd never hear the end of it.

"Gog!" she'd say, her long nose wrinkling. "Only brownies are thick enough to do such a thing."

She'd mean *stupid enough,* but she never uses the *s*-word.

Still, though I've banked a bit, I've never promised any greenkid an unspecified *something,* which everyone in the Kingdom knows is a totally stupid thing to do. If you promise a greenkid that way, you deserve what you get. Which is why everyone from the Out falls for greenman promises all the time, expecting to get something for nothing. Or something for very little, anyway. Outsiders—so my dad says—simply don't have the brains of a brownie. I've never actually met any.

Outsiders, that is.

So, there I was, trudging back downstream to our bridge, the cold water making familiar runs around my knees. The poster was rolled tight and jammed down the front of my jerkin. I didn't want the poster to get wet, which was why it wasn't in my boot. And I needed both hands free, of course. Even for a troll, river walking can be rigorous when the river is in full spate—and at the full moon, all the water in the Kingdom runs high and heavy.

I was humming a tune from the Seven Leaguers' latest CD, *TrollGate.* The part that goes:

> *Under the bridge,*
> *Right under the span,*
> *We wait for the night*
> *And the sight of a man....*

Booger sings this incredible falsetto on that one, sounding like a wailing banshee. No one else can hit those notes. I don't even try.

Since the river was running high and loud, I didn't expect anyone to hear me singing. But this one greenkid, who must have been lying down in the high grass, suddenly stood up as I passed by.

He called out, "Hey, Gog, wanna trade?"

I knew better than to answer him, and I just flipped a hand through my hair, the troll sign for *Get lost!,* and passed on. He was a greenkid, after all.

"I got a ticket," he called. His camo outfit was a dark shade of green, like the shadows under trees. He had a blue-jay feather over his left ear. "Up front at Rhymer's Bridge."

Which stopped me right in my tracks.

(Bad move number one.)

A greenkid can tell, just by the way you stop, what it is you want or need or are willing to pay.

Best to keep moving on.

But still..."*Ticket...Up front...Rhymer's Bridge.*" Those five words were all I heard.

I turned.

(Bad move number two.)

He smiled that patented greenkid smile, part charm, part pure devilry, and held up something in his hand. It was a ticket, yellow and green. For Rhymer's Bridge, all right.

"Wanna trade?" he asked again. The air around him shimmered and crackled, a clear warning that I ignored. Trolls avoid magic whenever possible. We can't do it, so we don't need it, as Mom always says.

I should have moved along—and fast.

Instead I gulped.

"What for?" I croaked.

(Bad move number three.)

The magic three.

I was stuck. Caught. Hauled in. Delivered.

"Whatcha got?" He looked meaningfully at the poster rolled tight and tucked down my jerkin.

I shrugged. One part of my brain thought that I could *always* find another poster.

The stupid part.

The part already under the greenkid's glamour.

I forgot how I had gone into the alley to get this

one. I forgot the alley's dark, dank, scary feel. I forgot
the green slime and the awful smell. I forgot the
sound of Mr. Standing Bones scraping himself together behind me, and how I'd run into the sun,
thankful to be turning grey under its rays.

But: *"Ticket...Up front...Rhymer's Bridge."*

The other part of my brain stopped working. The
part that usually warns, *Dumb move, Gog.*

I crossed the river, clambered up onto the bank,
drawing the poster out of my jerkin in one smooth
move.

The greenkid held out the ticket in his left hand
and I got close enough to see up his nose. No green
hairs. But then he was young, younger than me, even.

We traded.

Fair.

Square.

Or fair and square, according to the greenmen.

And in a twinkling the greenkid was gone, leaving
only his laugh behind.

I knew that laugh. It meant I was in trouble.

When I looked at the ticket, it was for up front at
Rhymer's Bridge, all right. But it wasn't for the full-
moon show. It was for a concert that had already happened, last week, Wild Hunt. They were a Faerie
fusion band, a rock-and-reel foursome: two banshees,
one on fiddle and one on flute; a guitarist with the
crystal blue eyes of a sidhe prince and a voice like an
aging angel; and a human drummer named Robin the

Adman. I had one of their CDs. They were OK. Good enough, though not a patch on Boots and his crew.

I'd been tricked, well and good.

But what had I expected?

He was a greenkid, after all.

I tore the ticket into tiny pieces and threw the pieces into the air, where they turned into strange golden butterflies that flitted away over the dark water and out of sight.

Will you go with me
Where the water swirls
High at the hip
And low at the curls?

— "Swirling Water," from BRIDGE BOUND

CHAPTER THREE

PLANS

It could have been worse. The greenkid could have gotten my pants or my boots.

He could have gotten my teeth or my tonsils.

He could have gotten my long red hair.

Everyone in the Kingdom knows someone who's lost such things to a greenman.

And the stupid part of it was, I knew better. I had known better all my life. But I hadn't been paying attention, because I was hungry for something.

Greenmen thrive on that kind of hunger.

I could still hear the greenkid's laughter as I slipped down the embankment and got back into the water.

The water felt cold. Or else I just was hot with em-

16

barrassment. I could feel every little whirl and swirl around my legs, and normally a troll hardly feels a thing.

I thought about running away to the borders where the Kingdom meets the Outside world. What was one more runaway in the dirty towns at the edge of Faerie?

Or I could run off into the great, dark New Forest, which lies at the heart of the Kingdom, a place so untrammeled and untampered with, it has more shadows than light.

But I hadn't the stomach or the nose or the heart for such places. Besides, my mom and dad would miss me.

Not to mention my best friend, Pook.

And my little brother, Magog. Who can be as smart as he is a pain.

Of course, if Magog ever found out what I'd done, I'd never hear the end of it.

So I decided just to go home and not say a word to anyone about how utterly stupid I'd been.

But word in the Kingdom has a way of getting around.

Someone saw the butterflies and figured out the greenmen had done a trade.

Or the grass on the riverbank told the lea grass. The lea grass told the meadowsweet. The meadowsweet told the trefoils at wood's edge, who told the catkins in the marsh. The catkins, of course, are notorious gossips, and they ran all the way up and down the river whispering.

That's the way word travels around here.

No matter how determined I was, news of how stupid I'd been was going to get home before me.

So, when I arrived under our bridge, there was Magog waiting for me on the doorstoop, hairless and smirking. His glasses reflected my unhappy state back at me.

I had to tell him the whole thing then. My side of it. So that he'd understand and put his hand in mine and look up at me with his face all shiny and rosy-gold, like he used to do when he was real little.

It was either that or have him at me all night long with his whiny "Whatcha do, Gog? Whatcha really do?"

I gave him the quick version first, the slow version after.

I sounded stupid in both.

"Boy," Magog said, "that was dumb." He doesn't use the s-word either.

How could I disagree?

"Tell me about Mr. Standing Bones again," he said, and he shivered. "Did he come very far out of the alley? Did you look at him over your left shoulder? Or your right?" Magog loves scary stories. He and his friends sometimes wear black jerkins and trews and play at being undead. They paint bones on their clothes with phosphorescent paint. They make fangs out of wood.

But then, they're *really* young.

"Were you scared, Gog?" Magog's little eyes behind the thick glasses were wide and he trembled with make-believe fear.

So, I told him the whole stupid story again, even though I hated showing myself up for a fool. Brothers do that, you know.

When I was done, Magog's eyes turned bright with pleasure.

Partly because I'd been stupid.

Partly because his eyes were behind glasses.

And partly because he had an idea.

"Since we don't have the coins for tickets, why don't we—"

"What do you mean *we,* bridge-bound?"

"I can go if you take me," he said. Which was true, since technically I'm an adult—I have all my hair. "Mom will let me." Which was also true. "What Mom says, Dad says, too." Three out of three. The magic number. "And then I'll tell you how we can get to hear the band."

My little brother may be hairless, but I think sometimes he's a genius. There's sidhe blood way back in the family on Mom's side, though she says that Magog got it all.

Me—I'm all troll. Big. Strong. Loyal. But not so

bright. So, I always listen carefully to my little brother, even when I act like I don't. It's a slow way to learn, but I usually get there in the end.

"Well...all right," I said to Magog. "It's a deal."

We shook hands. Palm-to-palm is sacred with trolls.

"We can set up chairs," Magog said.

"Set up chairs?" Even to me that sounded dumb. Of course, genius can be a pretty chancy thing and sidhe blood often runs thin.

"Carry guitars. Haul gear. You know—roadies." He grinned that big mossy smile of his. "After all we *are* trolls. Brawn R Us, as the sign on Dad's shop says. Haulage and Heftage."

That time I got it.

"Brilliant!" I said, and Magog's grin grew larger.

"Though we may have to go in disguise," Magog added. "I mean, we're not really big-enough trolls yet to do all that carrying."

"You mean, *you* aren't big enough yet," I said, flexing muscle at him.

"I mean *you* aren't either," he said. "Not really. You've got new hair and bumps on the arm, but there's no mass yet."

Mass is important for trolls. Lots of it. As Grandpa used to say, "Mass is mastery." I had to admit that Magog was right, though I didn't admit it aloud. Even I wasn't old enough yet for real mass. Troll mass. The bulk between the shoulders and right through the chest. Arms like staves. Thighs like trees. Massive.

But I did have muscle.

At least some.

What I said to Magog was "Unh." Which could have been "Unh-hunh" or "Unh-unh." Take your pick.

"But with a disguise..." Magog added.

Disguise. That's not a troll trait.

But another word for disguise is *deceit.* And deceit is what pookahs are best at.

"Pook!" I said.

"Exactly." Magog nodded, which made me feel good. Brothers are like that.

Of course, for that I had to make up with Pook, even if he didn't deserve it.

"All right," I told him. "But I go to find him alone."

"He's *your* friend," Magog said. "I'd never come between you guys." Which meant he knew that Pook and I had had a fight. Old news travels slow but stays around a long time.

So, I went over to Pook's house, though of course I couldn't go there directly. It's a pookah place, after all, and they tend to move around a lot—one day on your street, the next in an alley, the third somewhere way across the Kingdom. They never say where they're going, or when. Just up and go.

As Grandpa used to say of pookahs: "Light fingered and light traveling."

But if a pookah is your close friend, you can always find him somehow.

So, I did what had to be done: I stood on my left foot, put my left arm up in the air, and cried:

> *I call you, Pook,*
> *Earth to air;*
> *Come out, come out,*
> *If you dare.*

Of course, he came, with the loud snapping sound of pookah magic. He's my best friend, after all. He always comes when I call.

He took my hand and pulled me right through the hazy air and the sizzle of magic, and into his cozy little house. That's always the surest way to get there.

Just as well.

This time his bedroom was overlooking the Great Span, which is way over on the other side of the Kingdom from our bridge. I would have needed real seven-league boots to get there in time, not the plastic ones the hawkers sell at festivals to tourists. The only pair of real seven-leaguers I'd even *heard* of were in the Kingdom's museum. Well—they used to be in the museum. They'd been stolen over a year ago, and not even the Queen's Men could find a clue to where they'd gone.

"Are we still friends?" Pook asked straightaway, curling up on his bed. That's his usual opening line with me because he's always playing tricks. And I'm always having to forgive him.

It's a pookah's nature, of course, to be a trickster, though they are never mean like the greenmen.

Just annoying.

"Barely," I answered. Though truth to tell, I couldn't even remember what our quarrel had been about.

He nodded and sat up, his dark eyes full of sparkle.

Then we spit on our palms and smacked them together.

In the olden times, my father says, pax was sealed blood-to-blood. But one can't be too careful nowadays, what with True Humans traipsing back and forth across the bridges without thinking, bringing with them odd and mysterious diseases in their blood or on their hands or in their pockets. Why, the dirty little border towns are chock-full of odd fevers with names like Leak Ear and Droop Lip and Black Gallus and the Grippes. Even the sidhe catch them. The Queen had a cousin who spent all of last year down with something called the Spiny Pox.

So, we don't do blood oaths anymore. But spit is good enough. Spit in the Kingdom is a salve. A fix-it. No one in the Kingdom ever got sick smacking spit-to-spit.

"What calls you here?" Pook asked, grinning. He's

got a great grin, even for a pookah. And sometimes, when he's not concentrating, it becomes a dog smile as he morphs into canine shape—dog, jackal, dingo, wolf. He's got Irish cousins who do the horse/donkey/ass thing. And a great-great-great-uncle—so he says—who was into butterflies and moths. But in his immediate family, it's all dogs.

This time, though, he must have been concentrating, because he stayed in human form.

"Greenkid," I said. "Close enough for green nose hairs. Only he had none. No hairs. No green."

Pook had the grace to look embarrassed for a moment. "You were really *that* close?"

"I was *really* that close," I said.

Pook knew I was telling the truth because, unlike pookahs, trolls have a hard time telling a lie. Whenever we try, we turn this awful grey, as if we'd stayed out in the sun much too long. And I was as nice a pink as any troll would like.

I looked down and added, "Traded."

"Trashed?" he asked. He said it quickly, but with the careful tones of a real friend, though by rights he could have been hee-hawing himself into hysterics.

"Totally," I said.

"What did you lose?" he asked. He stared at me as if he could find a missing body part just by looking.

"A poster."

"That's all?"

"It was enough."

You could see him working that out, faster than a troll could do. He looked up, sly eyed. "Not a poster of...Boots?"

I nodded. "The whole band," I said. "The new one, with the color photo."

"Could have been a lot worse," he said, though it didn't sound as if he really meant it.

I nodded again. *Worse?* I couldn't think how.

"Could have been a *lot* worse!" Pook said, pointing to various parts of my body.

For a minute we were both silent, considering the damage the greenkid could have done.

Suddenly I remembered. "Magog's got a plan."

He looked surprised. "The hairless one?"

I nodded.

"A good plan?"

"For a troll," I said with pride in my voice.

"But it'll probably need a few special pookah refinements," Pook said.

This time I was the one who grinned.

Trade? Trade?
Got it made?
Got a pocket of stuff
That won't ever fade.

— "Trade," from BRIDGE BOUND

CHAPTER FOUR

UNDER THE BRIDGE

Pook took me by the hand and popped us both back through the dazzling air to my bridge.

We went in the side door, hoping to avoid my parents and explanations, but my mom's sidhe blood lets her know certain things, like when Magog and I are trying to sneak around. So she knew the moment Pook and I entered the house.

"Evening, Gog. Evening, Pook," Mom said, peering around the door and wiping her hands on her apron.

Pook looked hangdog at her, because he prided himself on being sneaky and she had caught us without half trying.

Sensing that, she added, "Stay for supper, Pook. I've got leftover amaranth stew—your favorite."

Amaranth stew. It's a troll specialty—thick and strong, without any fancy spices or spells. Just meat, potatoes, plenty of amaranth, and whatever green vegetables are lying around.

"Plain food for a plain folk," as Mom likes to say.

Pook's eyes lit up, and he accepted with a tongue loll. If it has to do with food, Pook's there.

"Ten minutes to warm it up," Mom said. "We've already eaten. Of course." She glared at me, her face saying what she wouldn't in front of Pook: I was late.

Again.

We nodded, Pook because amaranth stew really is his favorite and me because adventures always make me hungry. Mr. Bones had given me a stomach that felt like it had a giant-sized hole in it.

Ten minutes later Pook wolfed down his dinner, face in the bowl like any dog, much to my mother's dismay.

"Pook," she said, "have you no manners?"

"None at all," he said, grinning up at her.

But since he'd cleaned his plate—the green stuff, too (something neither Magog nor I can manage)— she softened, her face going all gooey and her eyes a deep brown.

"That's all right. You can't help being a pookah."

Then she turned to me. "Why don't you eat

everything on your plate, like Pook does? Think of the poor starving hobgoblins."

"Name three," I replied.

I was sent to my room for being smart mouthed.

Pook grinned at Mom, pulled his forelock, and ran to catch up with me.

"You never learn," he said, shaking his head so that his dog ears flopped in front of his mouth.

"That's not true," I answered. "I do learn. Just slowly."

It's not actually bad being sent to my room. My half of the room.

All my stuff is there.

And I was finished eating, anyway.

We played Boots's tunes on my megalodion. The windup is hard on CDs, but electricity is always chancy in the Kingdom, as power comes from inside the Folk, not along wires to plugs.

We began with the latest—*TrollGate*—then went back to the first, *Bridge Bound*.

I sang along, with my voice cracking on the high notes.

Pook sang, too, his voice sounding like the baying of a pack of hounds.

Dad had gotten me the megalodion last winter, in a trade with some mound folk whose barrow he'd helped enlarge. But the CDs I'd gotten on my own, earning enough by working after school with Dad in

the body shop, and all summer as well. The CDs—
and the magic cards—were where all my hard-earned
summer coins had gone.

I have twenty-seven CDs already, all cataloged. My
favorites—besides Boots, of course—are Richard
Thompson, Wolfstone, Boiled in Lead, and Ivo Pa-
pasov's Bulgarian Wedding Band. All of it's the kind
of music that's called rock-and-reel on the Outside,
but in the Kingdom we call it rock-and-troll.

Pook favors Loreena McKennitt, June Tabor, and
Shania Twain. But pookahs are like that.

As for Magog—he isn't old enough to have his own
taste. He listens to whatever I play, and seems to like
it. I'm working hard to teach him well.

Pook lay across the covers of my bed, half human,
half dingo, his long pink tongue lolling from his
mouth to show his pleasure. But he shifted to all human when we began talking about Magog's plan, because a dog's mouth has trouble forming words.

"The kid," I said, my head nodding in Magog's direction. He was fast asleep in his green pajamas, the
ones with the pattern of knotwork running up the
sides. "The kid thinks we should go be roadies. You
know: Haulage and Heftage. Carrying drum cases,
amps, and guitars for the band. Setting up chairs.
Brawn stuff."

"Brawn is good," said Pook. He got a faraway look
in his eyes, which usually meant he was thinking
about something tricksy. "But convincing the band to

use us when there are bigger and older guys around to be roadies will take a bit of finagling."

Finagling. It's an Out word that's perfect for what pookahs do, and they long ago adopted it as their own. It means to get something by twisty means. By tricksy means. By pookah means.

"So how are we going to *finagle?*" I asked. The word sat funny in my mouth. But then we trolls are a straightforward folk.

No lies.

And no tricks.

"Follow the Pook's lead," Pook said with a smile. "Have I ever led you wrong?"

I didn't reply. We both knew the answer to *that* one.

Pook spent the night, popping home for his pj's in a single swift motion, because anything Magog or I had would have been way too big for him.

Then we stayed up half the night talking.

Funny how the less you do, the more you have to talk about.

Magog was already snoring, that slow *pip-pip-pip* sound he makes, when Pook and I at last went silent.

Then, one after the other, we fell straight into dreams.

It didn't matter how late we went to sleep, we were up early in the morning.

Well before Mom and Dad woke up, we were already dressed, downriver—through a hole in the rowan fence that I made with my fist and Pook sewed back up with a spell—and under Rhymer's Bridge.

We were so early that we were there long before the three trucks carrying the band's equipment arrived.

And we were there long, long before those without tickets had come to stand in a snaking line, copper jangling in their pockets as sweet as the bells on the Queen's bridle.

And we were there long, long, long before the Queen's Men—in their grass green uniforms with gold braid and buttons, their wands in green leather holsters—came riding in to bring order to the crowds.

We were there when dawn drew her red crayon across the sky.

When the sky blushed a soft rose.

When the dew still hung like pearls on the tips of leaves.

Early.

Rhymer's Bridge is an old-style span of grey stones set together without mortar. On either side of the arch the grass is green as the Queen's dress, all year round. Under the bridge, though, the banks are scuffed and brown.

If you want to know who lives in the Kingdom, you read the tracks under Rhymer's. At least that's

what the ancient wisdom says. The old magic is sup-
posedly still there, in the hoofprints and footprints
under the bridge.

Boots sings about that:

> *Track and trail the long road home,*
> *Pack and pail, and then we're gone.*
> *Who can find us, under span?*
> *Just read the prints and know the man.*

But that particular tracking wisdom's been lost. Or
at least put away where hardly anyone can figure it
out now, except for a few old mossmen who learned
their trade before humans and the Fey started cross-
ing the borders.

When we were younger, Pook and I sometimes
tried to figure out who'd been there, playing Tracker
under my bridge until the light faded and we were
both called home. But it was just a game, of course.
Neither one of us—by sight or by nose—could really
tell who'd been traveling past. I'd never gotten any
better at it, but Pook grew into his nose.

We'd left home so early we'd gone without breakfast,
but not without work gloves, which were part of
Pook's plan.

"Never know what you might be touching" is what
he said.

I knew, and he knew, that he meant touching iron. For most of us, iron is quite painful. To some, it's downright harmful. For a few, it can kill. Gloves were essential if we were going to be roadies.

As we waited I drew in a deep breath. It was one of those delicately chilly mornings, with a sky the color of old pearl. Birds were well into the second part of the morning chorus, with blackbirds and larks competing for the lead.

About an hour into our wait, Magog began to whine, his glasses fogging. For a genius, he can sometimes be a pain.

"I'm cold," he said.

Well, of course, hairless as he was, he was going to be cold. I gave him my jerkin.

"I'm hungry."

Young trolls are always hungry. I shrugged and looked at Pook.

Snap!

Pook popped home and back for some tarts. Berrylicious they were. Even cold. And then, just to shut the hairless one up, he popped home again for glasses of milk. Well, for a carton of milk actually, since he couldn't have done his popping if he'd been carrying three full glasses. Pookah popping needs at least one free hand. And popping can only be done for three round trips in any one day. Three is a magic number in the Kingdom, of course.

"That's it," Pook said to Magog. "I'm saving the last pop for an emergency."

"Food *is* an emergency!" whined Magog.

We were beginning to be sorry we'd brought him, even if the whole roadie thing had been his idea.

The milk carton was one of those with a missing kid shown on the side. Not a pixie, like in the poster. This one was a young fairy, her wings hardly feathered out yet, with that wispy fairy smile, sharp little teeth, and big blue eyes under a mop of yellow-white hair. Under the picture it said:

> STOLEN: Windling, four years old.
> Last seen at Yarrow's Ring.
> She loves to dance in pale moonlight,
> And hear the night birds sing.

I covered the picture with my hand so as not to have to see her face—which was sad despite the smile—and drank a deep gulp of milk. Then I passed the carton to Magog.

He drank, too, and stopped whining.

For a while.

The sun rose slowly, and I thought about how humans think trolls turn to stone in the sun, which is plain silly. We just get grey like stone, instead of tan like sand. Shows you how stories get started. And then I was thinking about the greenkid and the poster and the tickets. It was all a big jumble in my head. Like I said—I'm troll clear through.

Just then we heard the rumble of trucks on the cobbled road, sounding like disgruntled giants.

Magog jumped up, waving his hands and screaming like a banshee. "They're here! They're here." His glasses bounced around on his nose.

Embarrassed, I grabbed him by the tail of the jerkin and jerked him down.

"Don't be a *jerk,*" I said. Which was three uses of the word. And if I had spoken them all aloud—and I'd been a pookah or a fairy or some other magic-maker—it would have been close enough for a spell. Of course, we trolls don't do magic. We just do mayhem. "Sit, Magog. Don't let them know how young we really are."

He sat but not happily.

"You wait here. Pook and I will talk to the road crew," I said. "Alone."

To make sure Magog didn't move, Pook laid a small holdspell on him, just enough to make him uncomfortable about moving away from that spot, though not so strong as to hurt him if he really *needed* to get away. And he added a smidgen of transformation, which made Magog look a bit like a pookah. The four-legged kind. A sort of cross between a fox and a feather boa.

Then we pulled on the work gloves and Pook laid a heavy glamour on the two of us. Under the glamour, my hair got redder and longer, my muscles filled out—becoming corded and knotted with real troll mass—and I put on at least ten stone in weight.

Pook—well, he got muscle and lost tail.

We looked older and bigger and much more knowing than we really were.

We looked swell.

In our grown-up troll disguises, we climbed the hill to the road, where the green grasses trembled in the breeze, just waiting to gossip about us.

The road crew were already out of the trucks and looking over the site. They all wore dark Levi's and black tour T-shirts with yellow lettering:

BOOTS AND THE
SEVEN LEAGUERS
Pay the Troll

"Hey!" I called out, startled at how deep my voice suddenly sounded. "Need some help? Brawn R Us. Haulage and Heftage." I didn't say anything more for fear of becoming grey with a lie.

They turned as one and stared. My voice *really* sounded strong.

One of the drivers, a man with a long mustache that cupped his mouth, laughed. "Roadies? Why not! We could use the extra hands. Work all day, and we'll give you comps for the show."

And just like that, we were in.

The rain rained up,
The Queen reigned down,
The horse reined in,
In magic town.

— "Rain," from BRIDGE BOUND

CHAPTER FIVE

ROADIES

There were six of them—four human men, a human woman, and a twisted little pan who worked the soundboard.

The humans all had those flat-sounding names that have little meaning and less sense: Joe, Mac, Stan.

One man—Charles Rudkin—almost sounded Fey but wasn't.

The woman was called Jesse Feldman. If she'd been of the Kingdom, she'd have been called Jesamin or Jasmin or Jasminia, for she had the wildflower look of a woman of the sidhe: petal white skin, with deep brown eyes so dark the pupils could not be distinguished, and hair the color of oak bark. But she

was a human woman, flat-footed and heavy with mortality, without a hint of fairy magic.

After they introduced themselves, it was our turn.

Pook and I hesitated. The giving of names is much more important to the Fey than to humans, who pass around their names with unthinking ease. In the Kingdom, knowing someone's true name gives you power over them.

Pook coughed and looked at me.

I looked down at my feet.

Neither of us said anything.

It was the pan who helped us out, though not without cutting us with his tongue, something pans do all the time.

"We'll call them Big T…" He nodded at me. "And Little T." He nodded at Pook. "For Troll. Terribly. Thick."

They all laughed.

At us.

Except for Jesse Feldman, who just looked annoyed.

We laughed, too, to ease the hurt. "Big T and Little T," we agreed.

The four men took the offered names, but Jesse Feldman was not so easily guiled.

"We'll call them that for *now,*" she said. "Big T." She nodded at me. "Little T." She nodded at Pook. Then she smiled a human grin, which was all but un-

readable, as it was made up of equal parts sincerity, self-interest, and greed.

The pan set us to moving the two big generators out of the truck first.

"Start with those," he said. "*If* you can." His voice was laced with sarcasm, which pans are really good at.

"Brawn R Us!" Pook answered in his new deep voice. He laughed, and the sound rolled out, mostly troll but with a bit of trickster mixed in. I hoped the pan wouldn't notice.

Then I *really* looked at the generators and groaned inside. They were massive, one for the lights and one for the sound system. Even my dad would have grunted once or twice shifting them.

"And get cracking," the pan added. "We have to do the sound test by noon. Playing outdoors is harder to mix than in a club."

The pan, of course, was too small for carrying and too full of himself for fetching.

Pook and I were to do all the heavy work.

But then, that was what we'd agreed to. We were roadies for the day. And everyone knows the roadies creed: *If it stands, move it; if it moves, get it to buy you lunch.*

"We're cracking! We're cracking!" I called out to the pan. But he had already moved off, muttering to himself the way pans do.

However, one look at those generators, and Pook

and I already knew they spelled trouble. We may have seemed like full-grown trolls—thanks to the glamour Pook had laid on us—but we were still only our half-grown selves. Glamour is only the *appearance* of reality, after all. Underneath the appearance we were who we were: One small pookah. One semi-small troll.

Pook got into the truck, put his shoulder to one of the generators, and started trying painfully to shove it closer to the edge, where I would haul it down to the ground.

He grunted and sweated; he pushed and groaned. He said, "By the powers!" loudly, not once but many times.

The generator didn't move an inch.

I got up into the truck and shoved the generator with him till it teetered on the edge, then I leaped down to be ready to catch it on my back when Pook gave it one more push.

"Spells!" Pook cried, his voice much higher than a full-grown troll's should be.

At that, the pan turned slightly and watched us out of the corner of his almond eyes. He lifted a hand and scratched between his little horns. I could almost hear him thinking that two adult trolls should not be having so much trouble with a simple generator.

"Don't look at him!" I warned Pook. "Don't let him see you looking. And keep working. If we can't move these things—and fast—we're going to be found out."

"The pan knows?"

"Well—he suspects something."

"No move, no comps?" Pook said.

"Exactly."

"I could pop the generators off," Pook offered.

"But that would be your last pop of the day, and it's a long way home after the concert," I pointed out.

He brooded over that for a moment. *He* could always shape-shift into dog form and trot off home when the last song was sung. But trolls are a slow-moving lot. Without the help of something like seven-league boots—which a troll invented, by the way—Magog and I might not make it back before morning.

And if we came in *that* late, Mom would ground me for a century. Half a lifetime for a troll.

Pook nodded. "You're right, Gog. Besides, popping would give us away. Everyone knows that trolls can't do magic. We don't want any of them—especially that nasty little pan—to know that we really aren't grown-up trolls."

"Terribly. Thick," I added, still smarting from what the pan had called us.

Pook looked up, saw the pain in my face, and nodded.

"Besides," I said, "moving something as large and

heavy and metal weighted as that generator would make a pop as loud as a sonic boom."

"Then let's get this thing moving *without* magic," Pook said.

"Brawn R Us," I said.

Pook settled his shoulder into the first generator and gave it a massive shove.

The generator fell off the truck onto my back.

And nearly flattened me.

A glimmer of glamour
A half-second's haze,
The heart gives a stammer,
The mind's in a maze.

— "Glamour," from BRIDGE BOUND

CHAPTER SIX

HOLDSPELL

My troll pride would not let my knees buckle entirely.

Slowly I straightened up, generator on my back, and carried the thing down the embankment to the shore. Pook told me which way to go since—bent over like that—all I could see were my feet. There was a strange popping sound from somewhere in my knees, and Pook had nothing to do with that. I knew I was going to feel awful tomorrow morning.

The minute we got the first generator down to the riverbank, the pan went back to tuning the guitars with a strange little device made of metal encased in wood.

All the while the humans were intent on their own

project and paid us little mind. Jesse Feldman was holding up a piece of paper and—squinting at the small print—reading the instructions out loud to her crew. Her voice had the authority of a queen's. Whatever she said, the men did at once.

"What do you think they're planning?" I asked Pook.

He strained to see. Pookahs have far vision, but we trolls are nearsighted.

"Looks like a floating stage," he told me.

"Won't it just float *away*?" I asked. "In the middle of a song?" I held my nose and made a sound like *glug-glug-glug*.

Before Pook could answer, the four men went over to one of the trucks and carted out eight huge iron anchors, which—with the help of rolling metal carts—they trundled to the shore.

Pook grinned at me. "There's your answer."

We couldn't help the humans with their work, of course. Touching cold iron is something no Fey can do with any degree of safety. Not even wearing heavy work gloves.

They knew better than to ask.

Pook and I went back to wrestle with the second generator, and after about an hour we had it out of the truck and down the hill, next to the first one. There we shoved them both onto the flattest part of the bank, beneath the bridge.

"Whew," Pook said, wiping his forehead, now

sticky with sweat. "I could sure use some of Magog's milk myself. Do you think he's drunk it all?"

We looked over at the spot where we'd stashed the kid. The holdspell was still working and Magog was nodding off, the shadows from the bridge keeping him out of the sun; he was a warm golden color still, and not grey at all, which would have given him away.

"No," I warned Pook. "Even the humans would guess we aren't what we seem if we quit now. It's not even ten A.M."

So, we went back to the truck and told the pan we were ready for the next job.

He looked at us aslant again, then scratched behind his massive pointy ears. It was a long moment as he considered our next task.

"Soundboard," he said at last. "Then power tap. Be careful."

"Everyone in the Kingdom knows to be careful around power," Pook said in his new deep voice.

"Wrong kind of power, troll," the pan shot back. "You got brownie brains?"

For a moment I felt sorry for Pook but glad I'd kept my own mouth shut. Which isn't being much of a friend, if you think about it.

Luckily the power tap and the soundboard were a lot lighter than the generators. Actually, Pook's house would have been a lot lighter than the generators!

We hauled them down without a problem.

The pan skittered down the hill after us in that rolling, galloping walk all pans have. It always looks like something itches them in bad places as they move.

Pook and I began to laugh. Then—afraid of annoying him—we coughed loudly into our gloves.

The pan was not amused. "Hey, T and T, when you're finished with the funnies," he said, "get the mikes." He turned away from us to check over his equipment.

"Where are they?" I asked.

"In the truck, sludge-for-brains," he said without looking around. Then added, "Trolls!" in a way that sounded like a curse.

So, Pook and I trudged back up the hill, but we couldn't find what the pan wanted. The trucks had been completely emptied out.

"What should we do?" I asked Pook.

He shrugged. "Ask the pan, I guess."

Of course, neither one of us wanted to do that. But what else was there?

When we called down to the pan, he trotted up grudgingly on his little goat legs—*trit-trot-trit*—and grabbed six metal mikes from where they'd been stashed. Behind the back of the front seat of the smallest truck.

"And what are *these*?" he asked. "Wands?"

I was impressed that he could handle them with his bare hands, but maybe he was used to it after so many years. Or maybe pans aren't so badly affected by iron. Or maybe the metal wasn't iron at all.

But Pook had no shame. Pookahs never do. "*You* said that they were in the truck."

"And what do you call this?" asked the pan. "A pumpkin?"

"I call it the *cab* of a truck," said Pook.

"You don't argue like a troll..." the pan said, cocking his head to one side.

I elbowed Pook into silence before he could answer back. "Just what our dear old mom always says," I put in quickly. "We'll take the mikes down to the shore for you."

The pan shoved the mikes at us. If they weren't iron, they were a good imitation. Because we were wearing gloves we could just about handle them.

Just.

There was one each for each member of the band to sing into and one extra for Armstrong's drum, all carefully labeled in a flowery script.

As we went down the hill, I whispered softly across the top of one of the mikes: "*You can always get something from a greenman...*"

My voice, with the glamour-added deep tones, almost sounded like Boots's.

Until it cracked on the long note.

The sun was straight overhead when the pan finally gave us a break.

"Get whatever sludge you trolls call food," he said, scratching himself again. "And then get back here. We've got plenty more to do. And if you do it quick enough, I might..." He glanced briefly over his shoulder at the riverside, where Jesse Feldman was gesturing to the men with her hands. "...I might have something else for you to do. Something that pays..."

"Sure," I said.

"What other things?" Pook asked. "What kind of pay?"

But the pan was already on his way down the hill.

There were lots of Fey on the hillside now, standing in line for early tickets.

Little mischievous piskies and pixies were the first comers, buying up as many of the cheap seats as they could. They chittered and chattered and did quite a bit of shoving, but it was more playful than anything.

Hunched knockers and bowed boggarts were right behind them, and their shoving was a bit more frantic and dangerous.

The night folk would be along later.

The Queen of the sidhe and her seelie court were sure to arrive last, of course, riding in on their jeweled horses just before showtime, and making a big entrance. But that's how they are. The horses' bells would jingle and jangle, the court would gossip loudly about the latest dances and talk about folk no one but they knew about. They would take up the entire front row, too. *And* they never have to wait on any lines.

Not like us workaday Fey.

But as Mom always reminds me, trolls are meant for hard work and we take great pride in it. The sidhe are meant for pleasure, and there's no pride in that at all.

So why they always *seem* so proud and standoffish has always been a puzzle to me.

I didn't see any of the greenmen. Not down where Pook and I were. But they would surely be working outside the gates until the very last—selling, trading, bargaining.

Cheating.

Someone—a lot of someones—was going to get skinned in a trade today. Boots's show was the biggest thing to hit the Kingdom this year, and the greenmen knew it.

The hill was now heavy with hubbub, and a couple of helpful hobs had set up stands selling cups of nectar and flower bread spread with gobs of fresh clover honey. There were gallons of milk, too, and from each carton the wispy smile of little missing Windling stared out.

The hive folk must have been working overtime to get all of that ready. We'd been so busy with the setup, Pook and I, that we'd never even heard them arrive.

I took a big sniff of air alive with the smell of the

food. I was hungry enough to eat a centaur. I'd even have tried some of the green stuff in Mom's stew. But I was ready to settle for whatever we could find at the stands.

We picked up a couple of pieces of bread with the few copper coins Pook had in his pocket, and headed for the place where we'd left Magog to see how the kid was doing.

He wasn't there.

The strands of the holdspell were twisted and broken, the ends glittering in the afternoon sun.

"That little nuisance..." I began. Sometimes he makes me so angry.

But Pook stopped me. "Look," he said, pointing. The glamour had begun to fade on his face and when I stared hard enough, I could distinguish his dog teeth. They were bared in a fierce growl.

So, I looked closely where he pointed and saw what was troubling him.

Magog's glasses were lying to one side of the spell, all twisted. My jerkin was tossed aside. The silvery strands of the spell weren't broken from the inside out.

They had been torn apart from the outside in.

Come to the Kingdom,
Kingdom come,
The will to magic will be done.

— "Kingdom Come," from BRIDGE BOUND

CHAPTER SEVEN

MISSING

I was stunned. I mean, Magog can be a major pain in the astrolabe some times. He can whine and whinge with the worst of them. But he *is* my brother.

No one messes with a troll's brother—and lives to boast of it. Trolls are clan folk. We are family folk.

Powers! Magog was just a little guy!

I could feel the rush of power to my hands and feet that we trolls call the Surge, like lightning shocking its way into my fingers. Some surges begin in anger. Some begin in heartache. Worst of all is when the two combine.

Suddenly I had the strength of ten. Or at least I *felt* like I had the strength of ten.

And I had the brain power of zero.

We trolls are total mindless berserkers when the Surge hits. As the power rushes to our muscles, it leaves our heads. Mass may be mastery, as Grandpa said. But the Surge is plain misery.

Except...except the glamour confused the Surge, and besides, there was no one to vent my anger on except Pook, which wouldn't have helped. Or the pan, who was working away on the soundboard, making hundreds of connections. Or the humans laboring under the watchful dark eye of Jesse Feldman. Or the gathering crowd.

Since none of them was actually the focus of my anger, the Surge faded away as quickly as it had come.

I took a deep breath.

"Wow!" Pook said, his hands up to his mouth. "I never saw you taken that way before."

I couldn't speak yet.

"My dad says to stay out of the way when a troll goes *splah*," Pook said.

"Yah."

"But you didn't rave like I expected. Your eyes got red, though. Red as your hair."

"Yah."

"Is that all you can say?"

"Yah." Then I took another deep breath. "Surge. Comes quick. Goes slow. My first."

"Your first? Wow!" Pook said. Then he added, "It's scary."

"Yah."

"So now you've completely come of age?" Pook said.

"Yah."

"You look almost normal again," Pook said.

I nodded. "Yah."

"I mean, the glamour has gone, too."

I glanced down at my hands. Normal size.

Glanced at my feet. Normal size.

Glanced again at Pook. He grinned his wolf grin at me. The glamour was gone from him, too.

"This isn't a smiling matter," I said. "My little brother's missing. I mean—*really* missing."

Pook nodded.

"My brother," I said again for emphasis.

"The nose knows," said Pook, pointing to his canine snout.

"Knows what?"

"Where the kid's gone."

"Where?"

"I can smell greenman," Pook said. "All around the holdspell. All around the ground." He gestured down at the area where Magog had been. An imprint of his little body was still held by the bent grass. The milk carton lay on its side, the picture of the missing fairy gazing up at me, her wispy Fey smile suddenly looking an awful lot like a warning.

The air grew hazy, as if bad magic were about.

And then I realized—it wasn't magic at all. I had tears in my eyes.

"A greenman?" I said, unsure. "But what would he want with a hairless, bridge-bound, nearsighted little troll? Is the greenman looking for a trade?" My hands made fists. I knew what kind of trade I'd make.

Pook shrugged.

"And did Magog get snatched awake or asleep?"

Pook shrugged again.

"Was the glamour still on him, or was it already gone?"

Pook shrugged a third time and his face suddenly closed down, as if he had a secret he couldn't tell me.

I thought about being a roadie and seeing the concert. Just a moment before, it had seemed the most important thing in the entire Kingdom.

Then I thought about Magog, maybe cold and scared. I thought about him trying to see without his glasses. I thought he might be hungry and hurt.

Suddenly the concert wasn't so important anymore.

"We *have* to find him," I said. "We *have* to get him back."

"But..." Pook said, "...we're just kids, too. Even if you did just come of age. We need to tell the Queen's Men. Give them the facts and—"

"We don't have time," I pointed out. "Look—the grass is already springing back. How long do you suppose it'll hold a scent?"

"Greenman's?" he said. "Not long."

"Pook, you have the nose right now. And I have the

troll strength. That's at least strength enough to fight a greenman. We could be trackers for real."

Pook put his head to one side, and for a moment I thought he was going to quit on me. "What about seeing the show? What about being roadies?"

"After we get Magog back," I said. *"After…"*

It seemed a safer word than *if.*

Going out to the wood,
If I dare, if I could,
If I want, if I can,
Going out to meet the man.

—"Meeting the Man," from BRIDGE BOUND

CHAPTER EIGHT

THE DARK FOREST

The real question was—which way to start?

Pook's nose was the deciding factor.

I shrugged back into my jerkin, stuffing Magog's glasses into a pocket. Then we headed up and over the hill, past the grimy goblins and the raggedy bogeys and the little tricksy pucks all lining up for tickets.

"Gog—hey, Gog!" someone yelled.

I turned to see who was calling me, and there, hands on his hips, looking cocky and sure of himself, was Robin Goodfellow, who I knew from school. As always, his grass green hat sat at a jaunty angle and his golden hair hung down to his shoulders.

"Need a place in the queue, Gog?" he asked.

"No cuts! No cuts!" a couple of brownies behind him shrilled, waving their hands about.

Behind them a group of beetle-browed ogres began to growl.

I brushed a hand through my hair. We didn't dare stop to chat in case the scent ran out before we found Magog.

"Maybe later!" I called back. Which quieted the brownies but not the ogres, who continued growling. Once started on bad temper, they were not an easy lot to stop.

"Come on," Pook urged, before dropping to run on all fours across the brow of the hill.

I turned my back on the line of Folk and followed him, my heart beginning to hammer with fear.

We're coming, Magog, I thought.

We're coming, little brother. It was not quite a prayer.

We're going to find you. An entire promise.

Pook and I made our way down the other side of that hill and up another, across short grass, through tall grass, and around a knot of daisies. We were careful not to disturb anything that could not bend itself back. Once away from the river and this far into the Kingdom, the Law of Harmonious Balance applies.

And if Mom's told me once, she's told me a hundred times, "Do unto everything as you would have it done unto you."

It's hard for a troll to be that careful. Especially a troll going at top speed. But I was. Because it was bad enough for Magog to have gone missing. Worse still if I did bad to someone—or something—good: grass, trees, flowers, or any of the Folk of the Air. That bad would come back on me. Harmonious Balance is not a law to tamper with. Or trample on.

Pook ran nose to the ground, and I followed. Once or twice he hesitated, looked around, and then—with a puzzled expression—started his search again. He didn't speak to me as he worked, and I was afraid to disturb him.

By the third small hill, I was tired and cranky.

By the fifth, ready to rest.

When we reached the crest of the seventh hill, I was breathing hard trying to keep up with Pook's steady trot. My legs were already trembling with fatigue. We trolls are built for strength, not speed.

Pook was still head down, and heading down the hill. But I saw what lay before us.

The New Forest!

Though why it is called so when it's the oldest forest in the Kingdom is a puzzle. The New Forest has borders with the Out on three sides, but the fourth side runs into the Kingdom. Deep into Faerie. Deep into the dark, untrammeled place where only the night folk live. Where wild magic still rules. Where the laws of eat-or-be-eaten still apply.

That scared me, and it takes a lot to scare a troll.

I called out, "Pook—come back! See where we're headed."

He slowed.

Looked up.

Stopped.

Sat down on his haunches.

Howled.

I caught up with him, and he was still howling.

Dad has told Magog and me many stories about the New Forest: about the laced-over branches that keep out all sunlight, about the souls of the lost sidhe who wander beneath the elms. He has entertained us with stories about the woodwives, who slip mysteriously through the trees on errands of their own; about the Weed King, who dwells in the inhospitable places on the edges of the woods. He has spoken of the shadow folk, the half-dead, the undead. He has warned about the wyrds and the damned. The tales Dad tells most, though, are about the Great White Wyrm, who lives in a lair in the very heart of the forest.

"There is nothing the Great White Wyrm loves to eat better," Dad always says at the end of these stories, "than half-grown trolls. So watch *out*!" He always shouts the last and pounces on us, which makes us scream, of course.

Are any of his stories true?

I don't know.

I've never asked.

Still, the New Forest was not a place I wanted to visit. Not now. Not ever.

"Are you sure we want to go this way?" I asked, trying to keep the fear out of my voice, trying to be casual about it. And not succeeding. "It's a scary woods."

Pook stopped howling. "It scares *you*?" he asked. "I thought it took a lot to scare trolls."

I nodded.

"My dad says the Great White Wyrm loves to eat half-grown pookahs," he added.

That made me laugh out loud. And when he started to get angry with me, I told him what *my* father had said. "He doesn't eat pookahs. He eats *trolls*."

Pook shook his head. "Pookahs, trolls—whatever. I just don't want to meet up with that carnivorous beast."

I agreed. Oh, *how* I agreed. "No White Wyrm, then."

"No middle of the forest, then," Pook said back. He got up off his haunches.

"What about the edges of the forest?" I asked.

"Edges are OK," Pook said. "The Weed King isn't much of a threat. And maybe a few hundred paces in, woodwives. And the ghosts of sidhes. But after that..."

I looked behind us, where the grasses were already erasing the traces of our swift passage. I looked ahead at the dark shape of the forest. "Are you sure we're going the right way?"

"I've been following the same scent the whole time, Gog," he said. "But suddenly the scent's gone wonky. I'm no longer certain whether it's greenman or grown man or something else entirely."

"What do you mean?" I asked, staring at him. Pook is hard to read sometimes, especially when he's in dog form.

"There are these strange shifts in the scent," he said, screwing his face up. "However, the one thing that hasn't changed is Magog's signature. Your little brother smells like no one else, Gog. He's definitely gone this way."

"Did he go willingly? Did he come by accident? Or—"

"There's fear in his scent, Gog," Pook said quietly. "Other than that, I can't really say." He pointed to the darkling woods below us and shivered. Then he sat again. I was afraid he might start howling once more, but instead he lay down, head on paws.

"That way?" I bit my lower lip.

"That way," Pook said miserably.

"Then *I* have no choice." I paused. "I don't. He's my brother. My little brother. But he's not yours, Pook. You don't have to come along."

Pook stood up, shedding his canine shape for a moment, and looked me square in the face. "Best friends,

Gog, don't get going when the going gets hard." He put out his hand.

I took it and shook it. I hoped neither of us would notice how cold and sweaty our palms were.

"Besides, you need my nose." He morphed back again into dog.

"Guess we go together, then," I said. "Edges and a few hundred paces in only."

Our first steps into the edges of the great oak forest took us through a shadowy patch where dark-coated Tamworth pigs were grazing contentedly on acorns.

When they caught Pook's scent on the wind, they looked up fearfully, and a few scattered, running away on their little trotters, squealing, "Wolf! Wolf! Wolf!"

But one huge boar who knew better turned his beady little eyes at us and snorted.

"Peace, old man," called Pook.

"Peace yersel'," grunted the boar. "Here in the great wood we be under the protection of the Sheel-na-Gig hersel'. Here all creatures be sacred."

"Even the Great White Wyrm at the heart of the wood?" I asked.

"Ain't ne'er seen any sech beast," said the old boar shortly. "Round here only the hunter's to be feared." He turned back to his food.

"Pigs can't see beyond their snouts," Pook whispered to me. Then he raised his head and sniffed.

"Scent goes that way." And off he went, in that lolloping trot, toward the darker trees.

"I heard that, ye young sprout," the old boar called after him. "And there be nae wrong wi' keeping mysel' to mysel' now, be there?"

"Nothing wrong indeed," I said, nodding at him. "So you're saying there's no such thing as the Great White Wyrm?"

"Dinna say that." The old boar's snout twitched. "Dinna say nowt." Then he bent back down to the acorns, and the rest was just the sound of crunchings.

Was there a Great White Wyrm or wasn't there? And did it really matter? We weren't planning to go into the heart of the wood anyway.

Just around the edges.

And only a little way farther in.

Then I glanced up and saw the dark running shadow of a wolf way ahead of me, down the hill, about to enter the woods.

"Wait!" I called out to Pook. "Wait for me!"

And without saying good-bye to the boar, I dashed after my friend.

King of the weeds,
King of the edge,
King of a kingdom
Of mallow and sedge...

—"Weed King," from BRIDGE BOUND

CHAPTER NINE

WEED KING

Pook didn't stop and I couldn't seem to gain on him, even running flat-out down the hill. Even when we go fast, trolls are slow. That's why one of us had to invent the seven-league boots.

Soon I had eased off to a trot, then a fast walk, and finally—when I reached the bottom of the hill and was just short of the woods—I just flopped down on a grey stone. My breath came in short gasps and I could feel sweat running down my face.

Perhaps, I thought, *I can rest for just a moment before continuing.* Something small and golden flitted by my face and I swatted at it. It laughed at me and flitted away.

Something else scrabbled into the undergrowth. I saw only a pair of long tan ears before it disappeared.

The stone wiggled beneath me.

I leaped up and turned around in a single fluid motion. Well, fluid for a troll, anyway.

"Who's there?" I cried.

A thin little fairy man, part grey, part green, goggled up at me. He wore a long grey coat fitted with acorn buttons. Green fairy wings, translucent, veined with grey, stuck out behind his hunched shoulders. On his head was a thistle hat. There were soft dark shadows under his eyes. Or rather the soft dark shadows *were* his eyes. His shoes were enormous, grey and slightly furred, as if he wore mice on his feet.

It was those shoes I'd mistaken for a stone.

"Take care, troll, or pay the toll," he whispered in a low, sad voice.

"I'm sorry, sir, but I didn't see you." *Be polite to strangers,* Mom always warned, and this little man was very strange indeed.

"Rarely seen in the green."

"Right."

"Hold tight, that's right!" he replied.

I nodded.

"I'm the King here, so we sing here."

"*King* here?"

His shadow eyes got darker.

I closed my mouth. Tried to think what to say that wouldn't offend. Maybe the pan had been right, and I was Troll. Terribly. Thick. But at last it came to me—everything the little man was saying rhymed.

Was I supposed to rhyme back at him? I strained at some sort of answer. But trolls aren't the rhyming kind. We leave that sort of thing to fairies.

And meanwhile Pook was getting farther and farther away. I needed him. Only *he* could follow Magog's scent. Without Pook I was going to be lost. Terribly, horribly lost.

"No time to rhyme," I said, and then giggled. I'd made up a rhyme without meaning to. It was an awfully feeble sort of poem, but there it was!

The little man burst into a song that consisted of chanting words without any kind of tune. As he chanted, he hopped around.

> *King of the weeds,*
> *King of the edge,*
> *King of a…*

I suddenly realized that what he was saying were the lyrics of one of the songs on Boots's first CD, so I sang back to him, "…kingdom of mallow and sedge!"

The little man clapped his hands and nodded, and—for the first time—smiled at me. It was a sad little smile, consisting of a twitch at either end of his mouth and nothing more.

"Dance and dancer, ask and answer," he said. Then he set a finger aside his nose.

Ask and answer. What did he mean? That I could ask him a question and he'd help me find Magog? In Dad's stories, strange old men in the woods often turned out to be of great assistance. But what did I need to know most?

Everything.

I looked over the little king's shoulder to the wood's edge. There was no sign of Pook.

So, now I knew the question that needed asking.

"Kind sir, my friend..." I hesitated, wanting to frame the question well.

"The end of your friend?" he said.

Oh yes, it would have to be in rhyme. This conversation was going to be harder than I realized.

"Listen, King...um."

Trolls and rhymes. Not an easy mix. Even Boots has to work hard at his lyrics. He said so in the article.

So, I struggled. *Sing, fling, ring, sting, swing...* "Uh... I need to bring..." That wasn't getting me anywhere. "Some sort of thing..."

Oh no! I thought, but I must have said some of it aloud, because the little king smiled sadly at me, this time showing mossy teeth. As if he'd suddenly made up his mind about something important, he held out a long-fingered grey hand.

"Woodbine and briar, to home and to fire," he said, touching me on the shoulder.

Before I could tell him that I had no time for a visit—only there was nothing I could think up immediately to rhyme with *visit*—we were suddenly surrounded by a strange green mist that made my eyes tear up. The green seemed to pick us up and carry us into an ever-darkening green.

When the mist cleared, I looked around.

The house was a single, low-ceilinged underground room. *Not much of a place for a king,* I thought. I was forced to duck for fear of bumping my head and ruining his roof.

Yellow and green roots stuck down from the ceiling and were looped and doubled over till they formed hanging chairs that were padded with orange and green cushions made of lichen. Smaller roots were twisted up for hooks, from which hung lanterns filled with fireflies. There was a blazing fire in the hearth.

"Um...cozy," I said. Then added quickly, "But not dozy." I smiled in what I hoped was a winning fashion. If you're a troll, it's hard to be charming. That's why Mom always warns us to be polite.

He smiled. "Cozy but not dozy, the Weed King's domain, where we are free of wind and rain."

The Weed King? Oh! That had never occurred to my slow troll mind.

He sat down and patted a seat nearby. "Come up and sit—my young troll wit."

I sat.

A wit? No one had ever called me that before! Besides, I didn't feel witty. Doing rhymes was tough work.

"House small. Troll...um, tall," I told him, reaching up and touching the ceiling. Things began pattering down on my head, including one very surprised pink worm.

The Weed King grimaced. "I like your style and big troll smile. Please stay awhile." He handed me a cup of something that was pink and smelled awfully sweet.

How could I stay? Pook was long gone. And little Magog even longer. The Weed King was a nice host and all—once you got used to his rhymes—but I was not here in the New Forest for a visit.

I shook my head. "Been fun. Gotta run."

The Weed King's shadow eyes grew dark and cold and very old. They looked no longer like shadows but like shrouds. Behind him the roots began to snake about.

I wondered if he were as good a host as he seemed.

It's never safe to mess with royalty, Mom says. *They're only loyal to their own.*

Besides, weeds are known to take over wherever they grow. And—I suddenly remembered—how my mother hates the weeds in her garden. She drags them out with terrible efficiency.

So, I remained in an uncomfortable crouch, my

head scraping the ceiling, and tried to look again like the witty young troll with the big smile the Weed King seemed to like so much.

At the same time, I was saying what he clearly didn't want to hear from me. "Kind sir, I really have to go. Er...my friend the pookah's not real slow."

That explanation seemed to work. The roots became still again and the Weed King's eyes went from black to a soil color.

Then he shook his head. "In the forest, without a plan, is good for neither troll nor man."

He jumped up from the couch and began rummaging around in a hanging-root wardrobe on one side of the room. All the while he muttered to himself in rhymes that I could only half make out. Something about *chasms* and *has 'ems, rain and wind* and *kith and kin,* and *a terrible gap* and *the need of a*—

"Map!" he cried triumphantly, holding up a tattered piece of moldy paper and turning toward me.

"Map?" I was astonished.

He waited for me to finish the rhyme.

"A map...for *this* chap?"

He clapped his hands together and a piece of the moldy paper spiraled to the floor. I hoped it wasn't an important piece.

"The forest plan—for you to scan." He handed it to me.

I took the map. It was as tan as the underside of bark, and as rough. I looked it over quickly.

There were three wavy lines that were probably rivers.

Several triangles I was sure meant mountains.

Three long gashes that might have been the chasms.

Then the place where a piece of the map was missing. (Was it bad form to grub around on the Weed King's floor to find it?)

And finally, in the very center of the map was a dark spot around which was drawn the form of a long white snake.

The Great White Wyrm.

"Do not squirm—go straight to the Wyrm," the Weed King said.

"Do you mean me—?" I began, but before I could find a proper rhyme to finish the question, I was enveloped once again by the green mist. My eyes began to tear up, and by the time I had rubbed them clear with the side of my hand, I found myself back in the woods.

Alone.

Woodwife of the greening grove,
I give to you undying love.

— "Woodwife," from TROLLGATE

CHAPTER TEN

WOODWIFE

I looked around. I didn't see Pook anywhere. And I couldn't hear him, either. No crashings through the forest. No twigs snapping. No baying. No howls.

"Pook!" I cried out.

There was a long green silence. Even the overlaced canopy of leaves was quiet, as if all the birds had fled the place.

I tried again. "Pook!" My voice echoed in the stillness.

And then I heard a small answering cry, more like a whimper, really, as if someone were in terrible trouble.

"Pook!" This time my voice came out in a whisper that tore like a rag on a nail. I turned quickly.

The cry came once more.

Pushing through thorny branches and reeds that slip-slapped against my leggings, I went through a little boggy place and over a stone bridge. And then under a great windblown elm that was lying half against another tree, I saw what was making the sound.

It wasn't Pook crying or Magog whining, but a thin and knobbly human girl. Dressed in a red knitted jacket, green bodice, and blue gown, her waist-length yellow hair loose about her face, she was lying faceup on top of a log. One foot was caught in the crevice of the log and she was trying to pull her leg out with no success.

A human this far inside the New Forest! I thought quickly, or as quickly as a troll thinks: *She must be terribly lost and frightened.*

I stuffed the map down into my jerkin and went over.

"Can I help?" I asked in my softest voice. Seeing a troll in the woods—even a half-grown troll—can be startling. Especially to human girls.

She looked up, her eyes glazed with tears.

"Is there something I can do to help?" I asked again.

I suddenly noticed that her eyes were so green, they might have been made of spring grass.

"Can you free me, kind sir?"

Sir! I looked deep into those green eyes. Swam in

them. Wondered if she was part sidhe, to be so lovely. I knew in that instant I would do anything for her.

"Just close your eyes, my lady, and hold still."

She held still, but her eyes never left mine, and the look she gave me made me feel strong and capable and fully grown.

I bent over and put my hands on either side of the log. Her foot was wedged in tighter than I'd originally thought, and the log didn't want to give up its prize easily. But I was a troll and strength was my greatest gift. I'd already been through my first surge and had unloaded two gigantic generators. What was a tree compared to that? My chest swelled, my muscles rippled, and with one great pull, I had the two sides apart.

"Draw your foot out now," I said sweetly. "I'll hang on to the log so that it doesn't close up and hurt you again."

She pulled out her foot, wincing at each movement. She must have been in terrible pain.

I wanted to hold her dear foot in my hand.

I wanted to count those sweet little toes.

I wanted to touch them with my lips.

I didn't, of course. I had to keep the pieces of log prized apart.

But as soon as she was free, I let the log go. It clapped shut with an awful *snap*.

"That's no ordinary log, then," I said slowly.

Duh!

Troll. Terribly. Thick.

"It's one of the Huntsman's traps," she said. "He sets them all about the woods to catch me and my sisters."

There are more like her? In the woods? I couldn't think why the Huntsman would trap them. I couldn't think at all.

She braided up her golden hair into a long silky rope and slung it over her shoulder. If anything, she was more beautiful than before.

Then I had it. A real question. "The Huntsman? Who is he? And how could anyone be so cruel?"

"He would have us love him only," she said. "But my sisters and I can't love him at all."

"Not at all," I whispered.

"Only you."

"Me?" I couldn't shake myself loose of her gaze. "But you hardly know me."

"I know you came to my rescue," the girl said. "What more need I know?" She moved toward me.

My tongue suddenly seemed terribly tangled. At that moment I wished I could braid my tongue up as she had done her golden hair. One part of me knew I was making no sense. The Gog part. But the other part—more like Magog—was whispering, *Think, Gog, think.* Only, who could think with her so close?

There were lovely blue shadows under her eyes,

around her mouth. There was a ghost of a perfect smile hovering on her mouth. I had never seen such a smile, such a mouth, such eyes. Such perfection.

"I mean—how could you—love me?" I stuttered. "You're a human. I'm a troll and not yet—well, almost—I mean, I—"

"Hush, my love," she whispered, throwing her arms around me.

What could I do but embrace her in return?

And then, in a single jerky motion that I could not control, I flung her away from me. For when my hands touched her back, I found it was hollowed out, like an old diseased tree.

"What *are* you?" I asked. A Magog question. It was suddenly clear to me that she was no perfection of a human girl but one of the awful folk of the New Forest, some kind I'd never heard of.

"I am a woodwife, of course," she said, her golden hair suddenly showing glints of green, like the reverse of a forest where the sun peeks through the canopy of leaves.

Oh no! A woodwife! What was I thinking? And then I remembered—I hadn't been thinking at all.

Her mouth turned sulky and she squinted at me. "Will you not love me?" She didn't sound heartbroken. She sounded surprised. And somewhat put out.

But her spell was already broken. Expecting a human girl, I'd reacted instinctively when I discovered she was no such thing. Only that instinct had saved me from her spell of love.

I shook my head and brushed my hand savagely through my hair.

"My mom's warned me and warned me about love spells," I said. Though she'd never quite gotten around to explaining exactly what was wrong with them. Probably thought I was still too young to understand. "So don't try *that* again."

"Mothers—we hate them!" Her green eyes grew dark, like the shadows under trees. "So full of unasked-for advice."

I nodded. That was my mom all right.

"Too bad, young troll. Too bad for me. But good luck for you. Who loves a woodwife, pines in the forest forever."

I shivered and forced myself to look away, away from her golden hair and green eyes.

"You did save me, though," said the woodwife slowly, "so by the Law of Harmonious Balance, I must give you a token in exchange."

I looked back. "A token?"

"But what to give?" She put her finger to her lips and stood awhile in thought. "What is that in your jerkin?"

My hand went up automatically. "A map. From the Weed King."

"You have luck already," she said, her eyes now the

green of new fern. "To be in the ever-changing forest without a map would have condemned you to wander for long and awful years. There are but seven maps in all, kept by the seven kings of the forest. The maps are rarely given. The Weed King must have liked you a lot."

"Well..." I shrugged. "He didn't seem much of a king, actually. And awful...er...lonely."

She laughed. "That's because no one likes him—scraggly mad old rhymer living in the dirt."

That seemed an accurate—though unkind—description.

"When you leave, you must throw the map back in or it will turn into fire and burn your hand off. Bet he didn't tell you that!"

I looked down at my feet. They suddenly seemed a long way away. "No," I said. "He didn't."

"Never *never* trust anyone in the forest," she said. "Not completely."

"Not even you?" I whispered.

She smiled. It was a lovely smile, of mist and sun and...She didn't answer my question.

"Is that advice your token?"

This time she got a funny expression on her face. "A warning is not a token, silly boy."

Troll, I thought. *Terribly. Thick.*

"Now, don't pout." She put a hand on my arm. "I was just thinking. But I have it now. My token will be to mark on your map the quickest route out of the forest."

"But I am not trying to get out," I said. "I am looking for my brother. My baby brother. He's been... stolen."

She shrank back from me and those green eyes became the color of the undersides of leaves.

"Stolen?" she said in a hoarse voice. "By whom is this baby troll stolen?"

"I don't know," I said. "Do you?"

For a moment she was silent. Then, as if coming to a difficult decision, she said, "If he's been taken, it can only be by the Huntsman. He's a horrible one, with horns and hooves and a hawk's beak. He eats small children and old women. He slaughters the rest and leaves them to rot on the forest floor. Worst of all, he cannot be persuaded. He cannot love." Her eyes were wide with fear.

I must have goggled at her, for she put her hand on mine.

"But you said he wanted you and your sisters to love him," I whispered.

She smiled that beautiful smile. "I said it only to make you think I loved you. That's what a woodwife does. Little lies inside a big one. But now I'm telling you the truth. You must get your baby brother before it's too late."

My head hurt with the circles of her lies. "Why should I believe you now?" I asked.

"Because now I have no reason to be untruthful. The Law of Harmonious Balance compels me. My token shall be a mark on the map that shows where your brother is being held."

"You don't know where that is," I said.

"*I* don't," she replied, "but the magic does." She held out one greening finger. "Take the map out."

I drew out the map but kept my hand firmly in place on the parchment. I couldn't trust her, but I needed to believe her.

She made a gesture with the one finger, a slight circling in the air above the map. Then with a light laugh, she turned three times in place, her golden hair fanning out around her head, her eyes now as green as grass.

And then she was gone.

Only the ghost of her laugh lingered, like a kiss.

When I was certain I was alone again, I opened the map. It crackled in my hands. A gilded X that had not been there before lay right over the Great White Wyrm's lair.

"*Oh, great!*" I said, my voice dripping with sarcasm. "Just great."

"I am indeed," said someone behind me.

I turned quickly.

"But you—you are the slowest troll in three counties. Terribly thick. And terribly thlow." He laughed.

"Pook!" I cried, mad as blazes at him and happy to see him all at the same time.

Wild hunt. Wold hunt.
Wind and weather.
Howl storms, break charms
All together.

— "Wild Hunt," from BRIDGE BOUND

CHAPTER ELEVEN

SMELLS

"Where have you been?" I asked.

"Scouting ahead."

"Edges?"

"I went halfway around, and then halfway around the other way."

"Halfway around what?" I asked.

"The forest, T!" He shook himself all over. "No sign of Magog there. Along the edges, I mean."

"Then will we have to go *straight* in?" I asked.

But I already knew the answer. The X on the map had told me. There was no doubt we were going to have to go to the very heart of the woods, to the Great White Wyrm's lair, to find Magog.

Pook nodded and his dog ears suddenly drooped, something that happens only when he's really unhappy.

Without saying a word, I took out the map and crackled it open, then pointed to the place where the gilded X glowed. I tapped the X three times with my forefinger.

Without asking where I'd gotten the map, or how I knew where to point, Pook sat back on his haunches and howled.

I dropped the map to the ground and grabbed Pook's jaws, holding them together to silence him.

"Hush," I said. "There's more out here than you know."

He stopped howling, so I let him go.

"What more?" he asked.

I told him about the Weed King and the woodwife. "And the Huntsman," I added.

Pook shivered. "Who's that?"

"I'm not sure. But whoever he is, he hunts woodwives with traps. And maybe other folk as well. So we need to be very very wary." I bit my lower lip. The unintended rhyme made me sound just like the Weed King. "Very careful."

Pook nodded. "That explains the smells, then," he said.

"Smells?"

"On your brother's trail. I got a bit of Magog and a

whiff of greenman. But there was…some other stuff there as well."

"Great White Wyrm stuff?"

"Could be." Pook shrugged. "But since I've never tracked a white wyrm, I'm not sure what one should smell like. The only wyrms I know are the small, wriggly pink kind who live underground, except when it rains."

I nodded, remembering the little pink worms that had fallen on my head in the Weed King's house. Had they any particular smell? I couldn't remember any. But then trolls don't have very good noses, not like pookahs' anyway.

"What did what-you-smelled smell like?" I asked, picking up the map again, rolling it, and stuffing it back into my jerkin.

Pook shivered again. "It smelled old."

"Old? What does *old* smell like?"

"Like cobwebs, only not so definite a pattern."

"Ah."

"And dark."

"Dark?"

"Heavy and deep and dreamless."

"Right! That *really* explains it."

He growled at me.

I growled back. "Make sense, pookah!"

"Something else, too. A different smell." He hesitated.

"*What* else?" I asked. "*How* different?" We were gabbling about smells and meanwhile Magog was getting farther and farther away.

He looked up at me for a moment, then shrugged. "You're a troll. How can I explain smells to you? It's like explaining colors to a blind man or sounds to a deaf man."

I grabbed him by the scruff of the neck with one hand and hauled him up till we were eye-to-eye.

"Don't give me that pookah guff," I said through gritted teeth. "Blind men can be told about colors and deaf men can dance to a beat. Besides, I *got* 'old.' I *got* 'dark.' So, stop the trolls-can't-understand talk already and tell it to me straight. This is Magog we're talking about, Pook. My little brother. And you know about trolls and their brothers, OK?"

He nodded.

"So, what else did the smell smell like?"

I was on the edge of going *splah* again and Pook knew it.

"It smelled...evil," he said, his voice a little shaky. "Worse than anything I can imagine. And you know that pookahs can imagine a whole lot."

I let him go. This time I was the one to shiver.

Pook sat down and gave his shoulder a hasty licking to show that he hadn't been frightened of me at all. It's a pookah thing, never admitting to fear. Trolls—we just get the Surge when we're really afraid, so that way we *can't* admit it.

"Well, come on, then, Pook," I said as casually as I could. "Just pop us over to the Great White Wyrm's lair, and we can surprise it. Them. Whoever."

Pook scratched behind his ear, then looked up at me. "And waste my last pop of the day, Gog? We may need it to get the three of us out of the lair quickly. You're being thick again."

This time *I* growled at *him*. The Surge really was beginning to well up in me. I could feel the heat rising in my cheeks, across my shoulders. I had to breathe deeply to control it. Dad had shown me how to fight it, saying, "Better than magic when it works." And it wasn't my first surge.

"One...two...three..." I breathed slowly, needing a clear head. "Four...five...six..."

Pook stared at me, ears cocked.

"Seven...eight...nine..."

The Surge backed down.

"Whew!" Pook said.

"Ten."

Then Pook looked at the ground and did his own deep breathing. "I shouldn't be telling you this, it being a pookah secret and all," he said. "But as you're my best friend, Gog, you've probably already guessed it by now, anyway."

"Guessed what?"

"Guessed I can't pop into a place I don't already know." He scratched quickly behind his right ear.

I pointed to the X on the map. "Well, then—know *this*!"

"If I tried to pop us there," said Pook, carefully, "we'd land *on* the map. Or *in* it."

"What?"

"Honest, Gog." He stood up and said, "It's Legs R Us for now, I'm afraid." Without a word more, he leaped ahead, going toward the heart of the forest.

Sighing, I followed. What else could I do? I didn't want to even think about what Magog might be going through.

Fear.

Hunger.

Torture.

Pain.

And him only a hairless bridge-bound kid.

My foot hit a stump that was iron hard and set my toes ringing. I caught my breath and whimpered. I'm not proud of that. But I think I was whimpering as much for Magog as for the hurt toe.

Fright.

Cold.

Torment.

Agony.

Pook heard and looked back at me over his shoulder. "He's not dead, Gog. Trust me. The nose knows."

Then he bounded away over a stand of large elms and oaks that obviously had been blown down in a terrible storm.

"Not so fast!" I called, wondering if he could hear me.

The pookah race loves showing off, and Pook was no different than the rest of them. He leaped, he bounced, he raced along, never looking back. All I saw was his tail and his ears flopping like wings as he coursed without a pause over briary clumps, mossy rocks, ironwood stumps, and rings of mushrooms.

Going deeper still into the New Forest.

We came at last to an enormous felled oak, its root system looking like the tangled hair of some dead god of the wood.

"This is all so strange, Gog," Pook said, nose to the ground.

"It sure is," I said. "No birds around. No—"

"I mean this scent. I get more from the air than I do from the ground. It's as if whoever stole Magog is now taking enormous leaps as he goes." He sniffed some more. "So what creature can do that? Surely not the Wyrm."

"Just keep sniffing," I said. "Who knows how much time we've got." I started to clamber onto the fallen tree, grabbing hold of some of the stronger branches to pull myself up.

Pook nosed out a narrow place and leaped right over the trunk. "Look ooooooooo—!" he cried.

Then he disappeared from view.

I scrambled up the rest of the way and looked

down, being very careful. We trolls may be tall, but we don't like heights.

Below was a vast pit that had been carved out of the peaty earth. It was not a natural hollow. I could see the marks of a shovel along the pit sides.

Pook lay at the bottom, legs splayed, unmoving.

Another trap, I thought, cursing the Huntsman under my breath. It had to be his work. What other pitfalls might he have planned?

Then I called out, "Hold on, Pook! I'll get you out." I had no idea how to do it, but I wasn't about to tell him that.

And I wondered, too, how much time Pook's rescue was going to take. Because time—unlike grass and trees and trunks and roots—was the one thing in short supply here in the woods.

CHAPTER TWELVE

PIT

What I needed was a ladder.

Or a rope.

I had neither.

I looked around carefully.

Tried to think like Magog. Couldn't.

So I thought like me.

What I had was forest.

Then I remembered a book I'd once read. A book I'd found floating in the river. A book from the Out. In the book a boy lives in the jungle and swings from rope vines.

Here I was in a jungle. Well, a wood, anyway. Surely I could make a vine rope. It had sounded dead easy in the book. Of course, I'd never actually tried doing any such thing. Not a lot of vines grow around our bridge.

So, I grabbed a green vine that was hanging from a nearby tree and stripped it. The thing was greasy, like Grandma's soap. And the vine itself didn't seem thick enough to hold a troll. Not even a half-grown troll.

Troll. Terribly. Thick, I thought.

Or at least, *Troll needs Terribly Thick rope to work.*

I grabbed a second vine. Then a third. By the time I had stripped them and braided them together into one long greasy strand, many minutes had passed.

I glanced over the rim of the pit. Pook still lay unmoving at the bottom.

Tying one end of the vine rope around a branch of the downed oak, I wound the other around my waist, tying it off with a strong knot. There was a little tail—like an exclamation mark—left hanging down behind me.

I looked again over the side of the pit.

Bad move.

There's a reason why trolls live *under* bridges! We really don't do well with heights. As I looked down, things began to swim around me and I got very dizzy.

"I'm coming, Pook!" I cried, closing my eyes. "I'm coming."

Below in the pit, Pook now was whimpering like a whipped dog.

I turned and put my back to the pit. Then slowly I began to lower myself.

Above me the top of the pit wall got farther and farther away. I guided myself by staring at the pit's side and didn't turn to look down again. I hung on with straining muscles, afraid to drop too quickly in case I should land on top of Pook.

As I worked my way down, I noticed that the side of the pit bore clear signs of a digging tool. Roots had been hacked off haphazardly; some were short, some long. I remembered the carefully looped-up roots in the Weed King's underground house. Whoever had dug here had cared little for the forest.

Pook's whimpering grew closer.

"I'm coming, buddy!" I called.

And then my feet—*hurrah!*—touched the pit floor.

Glad to be on solid ground again, I turned around. There was Pook, sitting up and in human form, cradling his right arm in his left.

"Oh, Pook!" I cried, going over to envelop him in a big hug. A best friend is family, too.

"Don't *do* that," he said. "I hurt everywhere."

I stepped back. "Don't worry," I told him, "I'm here to get you out. Can you hold on?"

He looked up at me, his eyes muzzy and glazed with pain. "On to what?"

"To me."

He shook his head. "I don't think so," he said. "I think my right arm is broken."

It *was* at a funny angle.

"Then I'll put you up on my back," I said. "And tie you on with part of the rope."

"I don't think so," he said again, then went silent.

I took his silence as a change of mind. And really, we didn't have any choice. He couldn't just stay down here in the pit till...

...Till what? Till the Huntsman comes and collects him?

I shivered.

"I'll try to be as gentle as possible, Pook," I said.

"And I'll try to be just as careful not to curse you," he told me. His upper lip curled. It was and it wasn't a grin.

With Pook tied onto my back, I hoisted myself up the side of the pit just one hand's worth, feet hard against the earthen sides.

"OK, Pook?" I asked.

"I think so..." he whispered in my ear.

Then, hand over hand over hand, I began to climb.

If climbing down had been hard, going up again with Pook on my back was all but impossible.

Muscles I knew about strained.

Muscles I didn't know about strained.

I got up three hands' worth, slipped back two on the greasy vine. Up three, back two. Up three, back two.

I didn't want to think about how I was going to feel tomorrow. But at least I didn't have to look down.

We were halfway up the rope to the top when—with a sudden horrible *snap*—the oak branch broke in two and we began to tumble down and down and—

"Oh no!" I cried. "Pook—look out!"

Pop!

With a sound like a clap of thunder, Pook popped us both to the top of the fallen oak, a place he'd been before.

For a long moment I teetered there, then got my balance at last. Turning around so that Pook was no longer hanging out over the pit and dodging the broken limb, which had been popped up after us, I cried, "You saved us, Pook."

He was silent.

"Pook!" I called again.

He still didn't answer.

Then, in growing horror, I realized what his effort had cost. We had no third pop left to get away from the Great White Wyrm's lair. And Pook was in no shape to help track Magog any farther.

Whether I wanted to be or not, I was on my own now.

I have walked five thousand ells,
And I have cast five thousand spells,
And I have crossed five thousand hells,
To make my way back home to you.

—"I Have Walked," from BRIDGE BOUND

CHAPTER THIRTEEN

HOLLOW LOG

I carried Pook away from the pit, still bound to my back by the vine. He didn't get any lighter as we went along.

As I was walking down the deer track, my mind was a mess of maps, pits, and traps.

How odd, I thought. *Only a few short hours ago, the only thing I wanted was to hear Boots and the Seven Leaguers play at Rhymer's Bridge.*

Only a few short hours ago, I'd been finagling tickets to get Pook and me into the show.

Only a few short hours ago, I'd eagerly put Magog into a holdspell and lied about my age.

And now all that mattered was rescuing Magog and getting the three of us home.

I had the beginnings of a plan. A slow-building, thick troll plan. But the only plan I had.

What I needed for my plan to work was a swift-running stream.

I took out the map and looked at it, but there was no water pictured nearby.

I walked a dozen steps, listened, walked on. The woods were incredibly still.

No whisper of wind fluttering the leaves.

No trill of birdsong.

No little feet scrabbling away in the undergrowth.

And no sound of running water.

Now, normally a troll can hear water from a long way away, and I was not hearing any. But we needed running water for my plan. So, on I walked, Pook getting heavier with every step.

Finally, about half an hour on, when I was ready to turn back and try a different route, I suddenly heard the unmistakable trickling sound of water over stone.

A stream! I thought, and headed off the path, right into a great green thicket. The tangle was severe; thorns tore at my trews and jerkin, leaving deep scratches in my boots.

Several hares started up, bounding away toward the path I had just left. And after them went a little mab, a fairy no bigger than my thumb, her transparent wings beating quick as a heartbeat.

Another time and I might have been stunned at seeing her. Wild mabs are all but extinct now. But I had no time for admiration. I was heading straight for that running water, and Pook was as heavy as a stone bridge.

And there at last was the stream, winding its lazy way through the New Forest. Tiny shards of sunlight sneaking through the green canopy of leaves sparkled on the surface of the water.

Safety!

I slid down the embankment and into the cold stream.

Trolls are always happiest in water. We don't swim, of course. We're not merfolk, after all, not selchies. But when that water swirls—"high at the hips and low at the curls," as Boots sings—we do feel at home.

I waded in up to my boot tops and was thankful when the water went no higher. Oh—I could have kept going all the way to my chin if I'd needed to. But water in the boots would have slowed me down considerably. And time was going far too quickly already.

I plowed into the middle of the stream, then walked along there for a good couple of ells to cover my scent. If the Huntsman used dogs, it would throw them off. And if he went by tracks, I'd leave none in the water.

All the while, I was scanning the banks, keeping a

lookout for a hollow log. When at last I spotted one, I climbed out carefully, walking only on stone so as not to leave footprints.

The log was perfect.

I untied Pook from my back and stuffed him, feet first, well inside it. He looked up at me mistily.

"Going to have to leave you here," I said. "Soon as I fix up your arm."

"What do you know about broken arms?" he murmured.

"Only what I've read in stories."

Even through his pain he looked surprised. "I didn't know you were a story reader, Gog."

I blushed. Reading fiction is not something trolls normally do. We read manuals. But Magog, with his sidhe blood, is a great story lover and he got me started. I hadn't even trusted Pook with my secret before. But he'd told me one of his secrets, about pookahs and their popping. By the Law of Harmonious Balance, I had to give him one in return.

So, I said, "I read a lot, actually. Especially adventure stories."

"I won't tell," he said, then passed out again.

I found a good strong stick and, using the vine, splinted his broken arm straight. Then I shoved him the rest of the way into the log.

Straightening up, I unrolled the map.

The gilded **X** on the Great White Wyrm's lair seemed to be pulsing. And near it now was a blue squiggly line that was the stream I had just waded through. Between the X and the blue line, about four inches from the lair, was a round brown column lying on its side.

The hollow log, I thought. *I don't remember it being on the map before. Don't remember the squiggly line either.*

"Thank you," I whispered into the green air.

All about me, birds suddenly burst into song. A brown thrush began, and a blackbird took up the melody. Then the tune was carried by a little rising lark. I didn't need to understand the language of birds to know they'd carry my message back—back to the Weed King and the little woodwife.

"Thank you," I said again, this time directly to the birds.

So, now I knew where I was, where I had been—and where I was going. The map was clear about that. I straightened my shoulders and took my bearings.

Due north from the hollow log where my best friend lay in pain.

Due north to where my little brother was imprisoned or hurt or...

Due north to the place where the awful Great White Wyrm waited.

I couldn't feel even a bit of the Surge inside me— no berserker rage to help me on my way. Just a determination that I *would* rescue Magog and come back for Pook.

Somehow.

And next year—if there was a next year for us—we would hear the band play rock-and-troll under the bridge.

Next year, with all this scary stuff behind us.

Little mab, little fire,
Touched by dreams and deep desire,
Grant me wishes, give me light
Take me home with you tonight.

— "Wild Mab," from TROLLGATE

CHAPTER FOURTEEN

OLD MAN
OF THE STREAM

I stepped back into the stream and started north-
ward, feeling lighter and—strangely—happier than
I'd been since entering the forest.

As I strode through the water, I could feel the cur-
rents around me, rippling and curling. When I came
to a still pool, I took a moment to breathe deeply.

Trolls are renewed by water. No matter how bad a
day, how difficult the trouble, if we put our feet in the
water, we feel better.

I could sense the water washing away my cares.

An ancient one-eyed grey trout lay under the
shadow of an overhang. He winked his eye at me and
I winked back. Trout and trolls are companions from

long ago. We share the rivers without so much as a quarrel.

"Hello, old man," I whispered. Such a great fish needed extra courtesy. My mom had taught me that.

Just then something skated over the surface of the water, a long-legged insect with green-and-gold wings. It slid along, entirely without fear.

Shedding light, the trout knifed up through the water and leaped after the insect. In a single fluid movement, he was airborne for a moment, then dove back below his ledge again, swallowing his late-afternoon meal.

What a marvel. He hadn't made a single false move.

I smiled and nodded at him, and he blinked back at me.

Trolls and trout.

I was about to walk on when I saw another flickering near the surface of the water. Not willing to disturb the old trout's supper, I waited patiently. It would only be a moment more.

The flickering came closer, playfully skimming across the river, as if unaware of any danger.

The old trout began to rise once again.

But this time, seeing what it was the old trout was going to eat, I moved even quicker than he. Thrusting out my hand, I grabbed up the flicker and pulled it out of his way.

The trout snapped at air and, flipping over, dived

back down below his ledge, but not before giving me an awful, cold glare with his one eye.

"Sorry, old man," I whispered to him.

But I wasn't.

I opened my hand and the little mab looked up at me, her tiny perfect face alarmed. Her translucent wings beat so quickly, they made a rainbow between us.

Trolls are big, and to a mab we must be mountains.

I smiled.

A mountain that smiled.

This seemed to alarm her even more, and she began to cry out in a tiny voice, so high pitched, so fast, and so foreign that I couldn't begin to understand what she was saying.

"Slow down," I whispered, keeping my voice soft so as not to add to her alarm.

But she kept on shouting at me and shaking her perfect fist and stomping her perfect feet. Then she opened her fist and began making signs.

Afraid the hand signs might be spells, I bit my lip. I had no time to be ensorceled in the woods by some furious mab. I needed to rescue my brother—now!

"I've just saved you from being eaten alive, you all-but-extinct piece of Faerie!" I cried.

She ranted on some more. Made some more signs. Light motes flickered around her head like a halo.

"Trout meal," I countered, pointing to the water.

She shook her fist at me.

"Look!" I said hoarsely. "Down there. In the water."

I could see the old trout watching. But the little mab never even blinked down at him.

Desperate, I put my face close to her and blew.

Hard.

She tumbled end over end through the air, then at last straightened up and flew off across the stream, making rainbows as she went. She never looked back.

I breathed out again, carefully, a long, slow sigh of relief.

Only then did I look down into the river. The old man of the stream, the grey trout, lay motionless below the overhang. His cold eye refused to wink at me.

"I'm truly sorry, old man," I said.

And this time I was.

I have walked through brush and briar,
I have slogged through muck and mire,
I have braved both ice and fire,
To make my way back home to you.

—"I Have Walked," from BRIDGE BOUND

CHAPTER FIFTEEN

THE HUNT

I slogged on a bit more through the water, putting as much distance between me and the trout as I could. Word travels quickly by water, and I wanted no trouble from his kin.

The stream turned right, going east as far as I could see. There was no help for it, then. I'd have to get out and plunge on north through the forest.

I found a low place to wade out and, just as an added trickery—some of Pook must have rubbed off on me—I walked backward out of the stream. If anyone saw my tracks, they might think I'd gone in here, not come out.

Now the woods on either side of the stream began

to darken. Overhead, the sun looked like a strange smoky orange ball. I glimpsed it through occasional openings in the canopy of leaves. But smoky as it was, the sun gave little heat and less light.

I took out the map again. There, as if colored in by a pencil, was a grey swirl that began below the left leg of the X and then swirled halfway down to the brown column.

When I looked up from the map, that same greyness swirled around me, like smoke.

Does the Great White Wyrm breathe fire? I wondered.

I knew dragons did. I knew fire lizards lived amongst the coals.

But does the Great White Wyrm?

My father had never talked of any such thing.

Trolls don't like fire. We're not afraid of it; we just don't like it. Fire and water are enemies, and so trolls—being water kin—dislike fire. But if Magog was captive in the White Wyrm's lair, then I would go there and brave smoke...fire...burning.

However, no one said I had to like it!

Rolling up the map, I jammed it back inside my jerkin and started off again along a deer track.

The way got darker still. In the smoky gloom I thought I could see the forms of fair ladies struggling to lean out of their trees.

Dryads!

Father's stories had warned me about them, too.

They look lovely but have strong teeth and nails. They eat what they catch. They eat it raw. I'd make a big meal for any of them.

I ducked away from their snatching hands, crying out the old spell: "Fair folks, stay in your oaks!" Though in fact some of them were in elms and some in alders.

Still, the verse seemed to work, even when spoken by a troll, for the dryads left me alone after that, only gazed at me longingly, hungrily, from their trees.

I walked farther along the track, scanning for what-I-did-not-know. This was scarier than the alley where Mr. Bones had been lying. Scarier than the Weed King's underground home. Scarier than the pit and log traps that had been set by the Huntsman.

I had a bad feeling about the dark smoky part of the woods.

But I had a worse feeling about what was happening to my baby brother.

So I walked on.

Suddenly onto the track bounded a shaggy lob, looking a bit like the pan who ran the band's sound system, only older, greyer, wilder. His little goat legs pumped madly, his scraggly locks shook, and he kept looking frantically over his shoulder as he ran.

Worried about what might be chasing him, I ducked off the path and stood as still as stone behind a sycamore. My skin was grey now instead of pink-gold—it doesn't take much sun to grey out a troll—and I blended easily with the tree. Since it wasn't a particularly large sycamore, my head was almost in the top branches.

I heard an awful baying and guessed it was a pack of dogs.

What pack would be this far in the woods? I wondered. *And who owns the dogs?*

These weren't comforting questions, so instead I concentrated on the sound.

After a bit I could identify individual yelps and yowls and yips and howls that blended into one long song of pursuit.

Like Boots and Booger and Armstrong, I thought. *Three very different voices and three different notes, but all somehow perfect together.*

Above that sound was another: a sharp shock, a *crack* like lightning striking.

The thicket on the far side of the track trembled and out burst the baying pack. There were wolfhounds and brachets, foxhounds and harriers, whippets and bassets, mastiffs and greys.

They were onto the lob before he could get off the open path. I heard his cry—shrill and terrible, utterly without hope—above their awful growls.

The thicket trembled again. Only this time what came bursting through was a man dressed in skins—leather trousers and a leather shirt with fringes. He had a cruel hawk's face, with a hooked nose and lips like a knife's slash below. There were gold rings in both his ears. A long dark braid of hair ran all the way down to the small of his back. Great tined antlers grew out of his head.

The Huntsman! I thought. *Who else can it be?*

Crack!

The Huntsman carried a long black whip, and it snaked across the path to where the pack was worrying the lob. At the touch of the whip, the dogs leaped backward, cringing and cowering and suddenly silent.

Only the lob's cries kept going on and on.

Two of the dogs—a stiff-legged mastiff and a long-eared basset—came crawling back to lick the horned man's boots. Instead of bending to pet them, he kicked them aside and with his right hand picked up the lob by the scruff of its neck.

The poor old thing was covered with blood and seemed barely alive. Unmoving, it hung from the Huntsman's gloved hand, except for a tremor in its right flank and a twitch of one finger. I could see the whites of its frightened eyes.

Quickly, quietly forming a circle around the Huntsman and the lob, the pack groveled silently, tails curled under.

"Got you, by the powers!" the Huntsman cried, his hawk face splitting into a toothy grin.

At his voice the dogs began barking again, this time a great knob of noise.

Suddenly the Huntsman put his left hand to his head and stripped off his horns.

For a moment I didn't understand what I was seeing, and I trembled, which caused the sycamore to tremble, too.

I willed myself to calm down, counting to myself as I would do for a surge.

"One...two...three..."

How could he take off his horns?

"Four...five...six..."

Then I realized that he'd been wearing some sort of hat with antlers attached.

"Seven...eight...nine..."

Underneath, he was a human.

And that was the strangest thing of all.

"Ten."

A human. A human had stolen my brother away? It made no sense.

Wiping his sweaty forehead with his sleeve, the Huntsman put the horns back on. "You've led us a merry chase, old thing. But it's to the Wyrm for you now."

The Wyrm! And suddenly it all fit together. In the book about the boy and the vines, humans collected animals for places called zoos. And those animals had to be fed, of course.

The lob started sobbing, then babbling in a strange tongue.

"Nyaaaaaah!" it cried.

Ignoring the lob's misery, the Hunter trussed it up with a length of rope. He slung it over his back like a piece of meat caught fresh for supper.

Suddenly, one of the hounds must have caught my scent, for its head went up and it began to howl.

I held as still as stone. Stiller, even.

"Quiet!" cried the Huntsman. "We've got enough. We're going home, lads. To the lair. This lob, with what else we've caught today, should satisfy the old wriggler."

He cracked the whip over their backs, and they ran ahead of him, tails between legs. As I watched, they turned north up the track, away from where I stood, away from where I'd stashed Pook in the hollow tree.

I pulled myself even farther behind the tree and went back to being still, waiting for a long time, long past the frantic beating of my heart, long past any fading sight or sound of them.

And then I went after.

CHAPTER SIXTEEN

LAIR

Trolls are big. Almost as big as giants when we're full grown. We've got red hair, pink-gold skin, and lots of sharp teeth. Some folk tremble when we smile. We keep our nails long.

It takes a lot to scare a troll, but we are not entirely without fear. These things can frighten us. Fire. Drought. Starvation. Solitary confinement. And dead people.

"Fear," Dad told me once, "can be caught like a cold, like a fever. And passed on."

The woodwife had been afraid.

The lob had been afraid.

And now I was afraid.

In fact, I was terrified.

More than once on that track—a *lot* more than once—I thought about turning back. Crying to Mom and Dad. Getting help. Those, of course, were sensible things to do.

Trolls may not be quick. We may not have magic. But we *are* sensible.

But then I thought about time. The lack of it.

And I thought about Pook, in pain from a broken arm and stuffed into a hollow tree, counting on me.

And I thought about Magog. Alone. The captive of a carnivorous creature of fire who likes to eat little trolls.

I thought about the milk carton with the picture of the missing fairy on the side. The poster with the missing pixie. I didn't want Mom to have a carton with Magog's picture in our icebox. I'd never be able to drink milk again.

So, one foot after another, I went on.

I had to.

He was my baby brother.

The farther down the winding track I got, the greyer the air. But the greyer the air, the less grey I got. The sun was not shining at all now. The leaves in the canopy over me were laced tighter than a new pair of shoes. By the time I reached the final curve in the path, I was as rosy as a troll should be.

But I was feeling very grey within.

When I made that last turning, the track suddenly widened out onto a road that had brown cobbles as big as my fist. I had to look down so as not to stumble on the cobbles or between them.

Long minutes later, when I looked up again, something big and black and monstrous loomed before me.

The great maw of a rock cave.

The Great White Wyrm's lair, I thought. I didn't dare say it out loud.

Drawing the map out of my jerkin, I unrolled it. The woods around me were so quiet, the crackle as I opened up the map was startling. I glanced around to see if it had alerted anyone.

The forest behind me remained still. There was no other being to be seen. I breathed a sigh. Not of relief. There could be no relief here. Not in this place where fear was king.

In the low light, I could barely make out the writing on the map, except for the gilded **X**, which was now luminescent and pulsing.

I drew in a deep breath, rolled the map back up, jammed it down the front of my jerkin again, and without thinking about anything—for fear of fear itself—I stepped into the cave.

The way in took a turn.

Dark.

A second turn.

Even darker.

Trolls don't like caves. Dwarfs do. Ogres do. Dragons do. Wyrms.

Now would be a good time to leave, Gog, I told myself. *To get out of the cave.*

But my body didn't listen. As if it had its own
mind, it marched forward.

One foot.

Another foot.

I shuffled along, my right hand on the wall and my
left jammed up against the roof of the cave to keep
from bumping my head. Surprisingly, for all that the
cave had looked enormous from the outside, inside it
was not even troll sized.

Suddenly, as if coming back from vacation, my
mind said, *What about that, Gog?*

And I thought, *Could there be magic at play here?*

Like a pookah's glamour? Like a seeming? Or are
caves just built that way?

Trolls are not great thinkers, but we are long
thinkers. We consider things slowly.

I considered.

And considered.

Not enough information, I told myself at last.

So I squinted and spun around, staring in four directions, one right after another. But everything was
still dark and I could still see nothing.

*Well, even if you can't see anything, maybe you can
hear something,* I told myself.

I stopped spinning and strained to listen.

This is what I heard:

a metallic *click,* as if a door was opening

a *whisk-whisk-whisk,* like Mom makes when she's sweeping

a *whimper,* which could have been from a puppy or a captive lob or even a little troll far from home

"Magog!" I whispered. Loud enough to be heard. "Magog!"

I took another step forward, and my foot struck something that went clattering and skittering away into the darkness.

I ran forward, scattering other things before me.

I galloped forward, heard a strange clang behind me, and...

...something troll height, but smelling musky and rank and sweet all at the same time, touched me high up on the arm.

Did I jump?

I jumped.

Cracked my skull on the roof of the cave and went down as if I'd been poleaxed.

High as a gibbit,
Hard as a bone,
Horned as a huntsman
Who's calling me home.

—"Gateway," from BRIDGE BOUND

CHAPTER SEVENTEEN

SURGE

I woke up minutes...hours...maybe even days later, in a chamber carved out of the rock cave. I could see, but only because there was a single torch somewhere above me.

Someone was bending over me.

I was so angry—with myself for being clumsy and stupid, with the Huntsman for being cruel, with Magog for getting himself taken, with Pook for leaping without looking—that there was a sudden rush of power to my hands and feet. I felt lightning shocking its way into my fingers. Suddenly I had the strength of ten.

I leaped up to grab whoever was bending over me.

I wanted to throttle him. It. Whoever.

I wanted to dig my long nails into his eyeballs.

I wanted to sink my sharp teeth into his throat.

I banged my head once again on the stone roof.

Strength ten.

Brains zero.

Funny way to be a hero.

That's the Surge.

This time as I struggled back to consciousness, I heard a voice I recognized.

"Gog, Gog, count to ten." It was my little brother.

"Magog!" I cried, sitting up. I didn't need to do any counting to calm me. His voice—and the hard stone roof—had knocked away any remnants of the Surge. Had knocked sense back into me. "How long have I been out cold?"

"A couple of seconds," he said.

"It feels more like hours," I said, hand on my head.

"Trollsssssssss," came an awful hissing to my left, "ssssssseldom thhhhhink."

Troll. Terribly. Thick.

I started to get angry all over again. Squinting into the gloom toward the place where the hissing voice came from, I could make out something large and white and twisty curled up in a corner on a big pile of stuff. It had many, too many, shining teeth and a long tail.

The Great White Wyrm!

"Get behind me, Magog," I said, struggling to my knees.

"But, Gog—"

"Now!"

"But, Gog—"

"It'll have to go through me first," I said.

"Who would want to do that?" Magog asked.

"It!" I said, pointing. Then I turned and looked at him in the flickering torchlight. Magog. My little brother. Hairless. Bridge-bound. I felt a sudden wave of fondness pass over me, quickly followed by a wave of pure annoyance.

"You're not that blind, kid."

"I lost my glasses," he said, "when I was bagged."

Then I remembered. *His glasses!* I reached into the pocket of my jerkin and there they were. By some miracle only one lens was broken.

"Here," I said. "One lens is better than none. Take them and look over into that corner. The one with the big white snaky blob. It's the Great White Wyrm, stupid."

"*Stupid?* I may be nearsighted, Gog, but I'm *not* stupid. Mom won't like you calling me stupid. And I know something you don't know." He said the last in that awful *nyah-nyah* singsong he sometimes uses.

I wanted to hit him, but Mom would have killed me if she'd heard. And he'd surely tell. So I said in a calm voice—more calmly than I felt—"What do you know?"

"Wyrm is as much a prisoner here as we are." He blinked up at me and the single torch reflected in the unbroken lens.

"The Wyrm—a prisoner?" I turned to stare at the white undulation in the corner. It shifted and twisted on its pile, and the movement gave me a sudden funny feeling in the pit of my stomach. I took a deep breath before asking, "*Why?*"

Before Magog could answer, the Great White Wyrm uncoiled itself and slowly, sinuously slid over to where I was standing. As he came toward me, he made a *whisk-whisk-whisk* sound.

Scales on stone.

My stomach turned over.

Maybe, I thought, *some trolls* are *afraid of things besides fire, drought, starvation, solitary confinement, and dead people. Maybe some trolls are afraid of snakes.*

"Ssssssssilk and physsssssicksssss," the Wyrm hissed.

I shook my head. "What?"

"That's why he's a prisoner, Gog," Magog said.

"Silk and physics? That's stupid!"

I knew that silk was pretty enough. Mom had a silk blouse that was the deep blue of the river in full spate. She wore it only on special occasions.

And I knew that there were some humans who studied physics in the Out. The Crown Prince of the sidhe—Prince Malapro—had gone to a human university to learn physics. He'd come back no smarter than when he'd left, or so I heard.

But silk and physics as the reasons the Wyrm was a prisoner? That made no sense. At least to a troll.

"Silk is the most expensive cloth known to humans," Magog explained, pushing his glasses up higher on his nose. "And by physicks, Wyrm doesn't mean he's studying about the universe, Gog. It's just the old word for drugs."

"Yesssssssss. Drugssssssss," hissed the Great White Wyrm. "Physssssicksssss." Then it whisked itself back to its pile, where it curled up again in a white twist.

I really *did* feel terribly thick then, and just stood there shaking my head.

Magog put his hand on my arm. "It's like this, Gog—the Huntsman keeps Wyrm prisoner here, feeding him fairy folk."

"Like the missing little Windling on the milk carton?"

Magog nodded. "Yes—only she's not been eaten. Not yet, anyway. Wyrm only eats on the full moon."

The full moon? I shuddered. "Why—that's...that's tonight," I said.

Magog nodded.

"But why so...so many?" I whispered, thinking about Magog and the fairy Windling and the lob.

"Well, Wyrm's pretty big to begin with," Magog explained patiently. "And then, the Huntsman likes to give him several choices for dinner." He sounded so...so unafraid. And I was sweating with fear.

Suddenly I remembered that clanging. Now I

knew what it was with an awful conviction. A door shutting. Behind me. I was going to be one of the choices, too. And I would make the biggest meal.

I shuddered again.

Then I looked around the cave floor. There were strange things winking and blinking up at me. I remembered the clattering, scattering noise I'd made, kicking something from me.

"What are those?" I asked, pointing at the stuff on the floor. I hoped that there might be something we could use in an escape.

"Treasures," Magog said. "The Huntsman brings them to Wyrm to make him comfortable. Gold goblets. Silver teapots. Aluminum siding."

"Comfortable..." I said slowly, then noticed that what Wyrm was lying on was more of the stuff. "He's nesting."

Magog nodded, adding, "On things of precious metal. And jewels."

"So wyrms are like dragons," I whispered.

"Exactly like dragons," Magog said. "I think they're cousins. Only without any fire."

No fire, I thought, *that's good.*

"Sssssssecond coussssssssins, actually," came the sibilant answer, "but who'ssssss counting." Then the Wyrm made a sound like a teakettle, hissing and rattling.

I shuddered a third time, then realized the sound the Wyrm was making was laughter.

"Wyrm doesn't mean to make drugs and physicks," Magog said, his arm still on mine. "But the Huntsman then picks apart Wyrm's cocoon for the silk. And the Huntsman milks Wyrm's blood during the cocooning for dream drugs. Then he sells everything he gets here in the Out."

"How long has this been going on?" I asked.

The Wyrm coiled himself in a corner. "Sssssss-seven timessssss ssssseven," he said.

"Days?" I asked. "Months?"

"Yearsssssssss," Wyrm said, uncoiling again.

I took a deep breath. I couldn't count that high. "And all that time you've been a prisoner here?"

The twisty white blob was silent.

"Wyrm is probably exaggerating," Magog said.

"Not by much," I suddenly realized. "Dad told me stories a long time ago about a white wyrm. And his dad told him. And his dad..."

"Probably not the same wyrm," Magog said. "A great-great-grandfather of this one."

See—sidhe blood. Lets you know more than you want to know.

"Have they been eating fairy folk all those years?" I asked.

"Well, a wild wyrm would eat less than a captive wyrm, because..."

"Well—the Wyrm won't eat *you*," I said loudly to Magog, as a kind of warning—though I didn't look terribly tough there on my knees. "I won't let any

such thing happen. Not to my little brother." I shook
my fist at the Wyrm. It made my head hurt.

"Trollsssssssss ssssssseldom tasssssssty," said the
Wyrm. It slid forward several lengths and then raised
itself up till it towered over me. It had three pairs of
jointed, clawed legs that clicked and clacked. Six eyes,
three on each side of its head, that winked on and off.

Any sorrow I felt for it melted away.

And when it grinned—revealing about a thousand
little pointy teeth—and flicked out its forked tongue,
my stomach lurched once more.

Lucky I hadn't eaten more than a couple of pieces
of bread and honey for lunch, or I would have lost
it all.

I have plucked the Devil's hair.
I have braved the White Wyrm's lair.
I have ridden night's own mare
To make my way back home to you.

—"I Have Walked," from BRIDGE BOUND

CHAPTER EIGHTEEN

WINDLING

Suddenly something white and wispy fluttered on little transparent wings into the light of the torch. It was too big for a moth, too small for a gull.

"Windling," Magog cried. "I *told* you my big brother would come."

The way he said that gave my fear a little shake, like wind through laundry on a line.

The fluttery white presence made its way over from the flame to me, then circled around my head three times before dropping down to my eye level.

She was a lovely thing. Her picture on the milk carton had not come close to showing how gloriously that mop of white-gold hair shone, how piercingly blue her tiny eyes were. Like all fairies, she had wings that were as transparent as glass, with small meandering veins running through, branching like rivers. She had the antennae that all young fairies have, shining like crystals of light.

For a long moment Windling stared at me, then—as if satisfied with what she found in my face—she took off past the flame into the darkness beyond.

"She's awfully shy," said Magog.

"And not much of a meal, either," I whispered. "For a Great White Wyrm."

"Oh, Gog!"

"Oh, Magog!"

"Oh, *Gog*!"

We were at a standstill. At home our conversations often went on like this endlessly. But this time Magog broke first.

"That's why the Huntsman went out and got the lob, I think," Magog said. "Because Windling is too small for a full meal."

"You're bigger," I pointed out.

"Well, evidently he thought he was getting a cat or dog. Because when he emptied me out of the bag, he said, 'Blast! A troll! What happened to that moggie?'"

I nodded. "Trolls seldom tasty?"

Magog nodded. "So off the Huntsman went—into the woods, I guess, to get something tastier. That's when he came back with the lob. He was a bit frantic, this close to the full moon and all. I guess he's had trouble with his traps lately."

I nodded and said, "I know about those traps."

He clapped his hands. "Tell me. Tell!"

So, I quickly told him about the traps I'd seen—the one the woodwife had been caught in, the pit that Pook had fallen into. He listened with his mouth open, gaping at me as if I'd been some sort of hero when all I'd done was bumble along.

But then something he'd said earlier began to bother me. I stopped talking and scratched my head. "Say that again, Magog."

"Say what?"

"What you told me before, before I babbled on and on. About the lob and about the bag and about what the Huntsman said." I was still thinking in my slow troll way.

So, he repeated everything word for word, which was eerie. He can do that sort of thing. Sidhe blood, not troll.

"Again," I said.

When he'd repeated it a third time, I finally got it.

"The Huntsman caught the lob. I saw *that*. But..." I said carefully, "I don't think he was the one who put you in the bag. Otherwise he would have known you were a troll before dumping you out." I was extremely pleased with my reasoning. Maybe I had some of that sidhe blood in me, too!

"Of *course* he wasn't the one," said Magog. "The Huntsman is human. He has no magic. He only has skill. So, he couldn't have broken the holdspell. But whoever grabbed me didn't know I was a troll. After all, he'd seen me with Pook's glamour on me. I looked something like a fox and..."

Only then did I remember the glamour. "And something like a feather boa." So much for my being part sidhe.

"But you knew that," Magog said. "Just with the bump on your head, you forgot."

I shook my head. I couldn't lie to my brother. Even though in this cave he'd scarcely see me turn grey.

But then I understood something else. "That means the Huntsman has"—now I was really excited—"an *accomplice!*" I started to leap up, suddenly remembered the bump on my head, and forced myself to stand carefully. "So that means..."

And just as I was about to put the whole thing together—every part of it—there came a faraway groan.

"The lob," whispered Magog. "I picked him up and carried him around the corner into the other chamber, hoping Wyrm wouldn't smell him. Blood probably excites him. It does dragons. And the lob was all bloody, poor thing. And afterward I pulled you in, too. You're lots heavier than the lob."

"And now," I told him—still being slow and careful about everything—"you're all bloody, too."

For the first time Magog looked scared. He glanced down at his clothes, at the dark patches on his jerkin.

I slipped off my own jerkin, jamming the map down the front of my trews. "You'd better wear this. And take yours off. We'll get rid of it around a corner or something."

My jerkin was miles too big for him. He's pretty small for a troll. The bottom came down past his knees.

"That's better," I said.

"Not much of a disguise," he said. He shrugged and tried to look brave. "It doesn't matter. Wyrms don't find trolls all that good to eat. Besides, *you'd* make more of a meal than me."

"*Much* more of a meal," I said heartily, trying to keep up his spirits.

But he broke down and began crying. "What are we going to do, Gog? What are we going to do?"

"We're going to get out of here," I said with more certainty than I felt. "Before moonrise."

"And take Windling and the lob with us?" he asked. I could still hear tears in his voice.

"Of course," I said. "What kind of a Kingdomer do you think I'd be if I left them behind?"

"You're the best!" he said, and threw his arms around me.

Lucky it was dark and I had my back to the torch, or he would have seen me blush. Blushing is not something trolls do often. Or well.

Just then Windling returned, circling and circling the light, and this time she was twittering.

"Slow down," I told her, and made a motion with my hand. When fairies get excited, they talk fast. And when they talk fast, they sound a lot like my megalodion on its highest speed.

She took a deep breath and came over to me. Hovering in front of my face, she said in a high little voice:

> *Here…here comes Huntsman*
> *With his knife*
> *To give the White Wyrm*
> *Life for life.*

Then she spun away, twittering and zigzagging in front of the torchlight and throwing wild shadows onto the stone walls.

"What can we do, Gog?" cried my little brother.

"Shut up—I'm trying to think," I said, thinking only, *Troll. Terribly. Thick.*

The White Wyrm began to slide toward us again, its scales *whisk-whisk-whisk*ing on the stone floor.

I feel the rage,
I sense the urge.
The lightning strike
That is the Surge.

—"Surge," from TROLLGATE

CHAPTER NINETEEN

FEEDING TIME

I tried to think. Really, I did.

But Magog was crying.

Windling was twittering.

The lob was whimpering.

The Wyrm was *whisk-whisk*ing.

And then the iron door opened and clanged shut behind the Huntsman. His footsteps echoed coldly on the stone, coming in our direction.

No one could have done much thinking in all that racket. Especially not a troll. So, I stopped thinking and shrank back against the wall, trying to disguise myself in the shadows. Hoping that a big surprise like a troll—well, at least a half-grown surprise—might scare the Huntsman into letting us all go.

In came the hawk-faced Huntsman, and this time he was not wearing his horned helmet. He carried a dirk with a jagged edge in his right hand, an enormous rope net over his shoulder.

"Feeding time, Wyrm," he called, and his voice was as cruel as his face. "Time to eat and to make your cocoon."

He grabbed Wyrm's tail with his left hand and pulled it backward so that the scales sliding over the stone made an odd, troubling sound.

"Sssssstop, Huntsssssssman!" cried Wyrm, trying to pull away. Its body curved like a big **S**.

The Huntsman put the dirk between his teeth, then grabbed the net off his shoulder and lofted it, twirling it around three times, without ever letting loose of the Wyrm's tail. Then he threw the net over the Wyrm's uplifted head and laughed.

"Don't want you to get any ideas about *me,* Wyrm," he said. He spoke softly, a harsh whisper, which seemed—somehow—more powerful. "I know your true name. You don't know mine. Remember which way the power flows."

The moment the net touched its head, the Wyrm began to twist and turn. But that seemed only to set the net more firmly around it. Still, Wyrm kept writhing and wriggling until it was entirely entangled. At last—exhausted—it lay on the cave floor, its unblinking eyes staring up at its captor.

With three quick slices of his knife, the Huntsman freed Wyrm's head, but the rest of the creature he left caught in the net.

Only then did the Huntsman look around, spotting Magog, who had been too scared to move into the shadows with me.

"Well, little troll, and where's that lob got to, eh?" he asked. Now his voice was low and sweet, which made everything he said sound even nastier.

I was not the only one who shivered.

"If you show me, I may let you live a little while longer. Wyrms don't like trolls much, anyway. Something to do with the taste, I've found. But in the end, if there's not much else, Wyrm will forget its disinclinations and eat you, too."

Magog whimpered, sounding more like a human than the little hairless troll I knew. I could tell that the Huntsman had scared him. Powers. The man scared me, too.

The Huntsman smiled and the light of the torch made his teeth gleam horribly. "If it doesn't eat you this full moon, little troll, then it may eat you next. But that's a whole month more of living. Surely, you want to live a month more! Just tell me where that lob went to. I don't have much time. If Wyrm doesn't eat at moonrise, it won't make its cocoon. My people won't like that much. So it's you or the lob. Your choice, little troll." The Huntsman leaned over and grabbed Magog up by one leg. "Better talk soon." He began swinging Magog closer and closer to Wyrm's head.

What an awful choice. For a second I was glad I didn't have to make it, then realized what I was thinking.

Upside down, Magog suddenly started crying out loud and wiped his dripping nose with the back of his hand.

Nobody makes my little brother cry but me! I thought, which is really the only kind of thinking trolls do.

And then I felt lightning shocking up through my body: feet, ankles, knees, thighs, fingers, hands, arms. Anger and fear and heartache all combined. The Surge.

"YAAAAAH!" I screamed, and leaped out: a big, hairy, thundering shadow where the Huntsman least expected one.

Still, the Huntsman was a strong, experienced fighter. And he had a knife. Quickly turning to face me, his stance sure, he dropped Magog onto the floor and never stopped smiling.

The Surge didn't let me worry about any of that, though. It didn't let me worry about *anything*. I simply ran straight at the Huntsman, my arms wide.

"YAAAAAH!" I screamed again.

The knife flashed upward.

I tripped over Magog, slipped on something else,

then fell forward, and the weight of my body crushed the Huntsman against the hard stone wall.

He struck at me with the knife and I felt it cut deep into my shoulder.

I should have felt it burning. Cold iron in Fey flesh.

But I felt no pain.

No fear.

No caution.

Nothing.

I was caught up in the Surge.

"YAAAAAH!"

The knife went deeper and deeper still, and then suddenly somebody let out a scream.

I knew it wasn't me.

The scream went on and on.

I *thought* it wasn't me.

The scream was high.

My voice is low.

"YAAAAAH!"

The Huntsman screamed again and then he cried out in agony, "You little—"

Now, I'm not little. Even in the midst of the Surge I knew that much. Ferocious in my rage, I glared at the Huntsman.

At the knife in my shoulder.

At Magog's teeth in the Huntsman's knife hand.

"YAAAAAH!" I pounded my fist into the Huntsman's face.

He let go of the knife.

"YAAAAAH!" I butted my head into his stomach.

He let go of his dinner.

"YAAAAAH!" I stomped on his head.

He let go of everything.

I lifted his limp, unconscious body up and flung him over my back, then sat down as the Surge slowly seeped away.

*One...two...three...*I thought.

I heard an awful crunching behind me.

Four...five...six...

I didn't want to turn around.

Seven...eight...nine...

But slowly I did.

Ten.

Boy, did my shoulder hurt.

But, boy! That was nothing compared to the way the Huntsman must have been feeling.

If he could still feel anything.

All that was left of him was a pair of legs sticking out of the Great White Wyrm's uncovered mouth. A pair of legs and feet clad in dark leather boots.

A miracle had started inside that entanglement. Still covered with the netting, the Great White Wyrm began spinning its cocoon with long white silk as soft and as strong as dreams.

Spin and spin the magic spell
Till all the story's bound up well.

—"Wyrm," from TROLLGATE

CHAPTER TWENTY

COCOON

In the flickering torchlight, we watched the white silk thread run out of a tube under the Wyrm's mouth, near where the last of the Huntsman's boots was disappearing. The silk threaded its way on the inside of the netting and wrapped the Wyrm up in an ever-growing white cocoon that looked like bedsheets dipped in mortar.

"Funny, that," said Magog.

"What?" It was all I could manage yet.

"That something so beautiful can come from something so scary."

"Milk...from...cows," I said. "And wool...from... sheep."

Magog laughed. Then he looked at me. "How's that shoulder, big brother?"

I groaned.

Windling twittered.

"We have to get home," Magog said, "and get your shoulder bandaged."

Slowly I stood, though Magog had to help me.

"Door," I said.

He took the torch from its holder and we walked down one of the stone corridors till we got to the iron door. It was built flush into the stone and had deep carvings on it of a Wild Hunt. The horned man, the dogs, a near-naked woman who was part deer running from them. It was unsettling, like too much dark chocolate.

The iron door was locked.

Tight.

I couldn't summon even a bit of the Surge to try and knock it over. And without the Surge, I didn't even dare touch it.

Iron.

Cold iron.

That burns the Fey.

"Key?" I asked.

Fluttering near the torch, Windling began her twittering again.

"Slow...!" I said.

She slowed down. Or at least to as slow as a fairy can go, and in her high little voice said:

Huntsman's key
Is in cocoon.
Inside out
It will be soon.

"What?" The end of the Surge and the pain in my shoulder kept me from speaking any more than that. *Why can't fairies speak straight?* I thought. *Like trolls?*

"The key was probably in the Huntsman's pocket," said Magog. He shifted the glasses up his nose again. "And the Huntsman is in…" His face suddenly paled, like an old moon.

"…Wyrm," I said.

"…the cocoon," he finished. He put his hand in mine and looked up at me, his face all shiny.

None of us wanted to go back to the chamber where Wyrm was spinning his silken shroud. Instead we went to check up on the old shaggy lob.

He was sitting up, looking frightened but very much alive. One of his little horns had been broken in the fight with the dogs, and it had jagged sides and a bit of marrow showing. There were deep toothmarks on his arms and shoulders. The fur on his goat legs was patchy and torn. He was a mess. But lobs, even at the best of times, are a mess.

"It's all right, old one," I said, language returning to me at last. "The Great White Wyrm has fed."

He stood up on his dirty little hooves, eyes still moist with terror.

"Nyaaaah, nyaaaah, nyaaaah," he said, sounding just like a goat.

"He doesn't really speak," Magog told me.

"He doesn't have to," I said. "We all know what he means."

There was nowhere else to go. The cave was essentially five chambers—one large and four small—with a single narrow entry, guarded by the iron door.

Once we had explored the lob's chamber, the three smaller rooms, and the corridor—with the litter of boots, hats, jewels, jerkins, leather bags, reed baskets, gold coins—we were left with the Great White Wyrm's lair.

"I'll go in first," I whispered.

Magog, the lob, and Windling trailed behind.

I stuck my head around the curved stone entry, holding the torch up in front of me.

I am not sure what I expected. But the room was absolutely quiet. From the ceiling hung a giant cocoon. What had been the long, snaky Wyrm was now a great silken bag still entangled in the netting.

"Good-bye, key," I said, stepping into the room.

"Good-bye, Huntsman," Magog added.

"Nyaaaah, nyaaaah, nyaaaah," said the shaggy lob.

Windling began to circle the bottom end of the hanging cocoon, crying in her twittery voice:

> *Soon,*
> *Cocoon,*
> *Soon.*

It didn't take a genius to figure out what she meant by that.

I found the Huntsman's knife on the floor, picked it up by its wooden handle, and went over to the cocoon. Fighting down my fear, I sawed away at the ropes until all the pieces were gone. Then I sat down with the others to watch what would happen.

We waited for long minutes, maybe hours. And finally, with a sound like cloth tearing on a nail, a jagged line began to run slowly across the silken bottom.

The line grew thicker, deeper.

Became a crack.

A crevice.

A chasm.

Something began to push its way through the opening, something dark and leathery.

"The Huntsman's boots!" Magog cried.

"Not terribly tasty?" I asked.

"Nyaaaah, nyaaaah, nyaaaah." The lob's comment said it all.

Something else dropped through the hole.

"His belt," I cried.

Then something small and shiny clattered to the cave floor.

"The key!" Magog cried.

Together we dove for the key and touched it. We tried to pick it up.

It burned, burned, burned in our hands.

We dropped it.

The lob trotted over, carrying Magog's bloody jerkin. "Nyaaaah," he said.

Using the jerkin to shield my fingers, I picked up the key and ran out the chamber, down the dark and twisty corridor, to the door.

Magog followed right behind, carrying the torch in both hands.

Carefully I inserted the key into the lock and— using Magog's jerkin again—pushed the iron door open.

A rush of fresh air greeted us, nearly guttering the torch.

A rush of wings overhead nearly put it out as well.

We looked up. Above us flew a gigantic butterfly with light green wings veined with orange and olive.

"Free!" it cried in a voice that was both beautiful and fierce. "Free at lasssst."

As it passed over me, I saw that it was grinning, revealing about a thousand pointy teeth.

"How about a little thanks!" I called after it. But I was glad that it didn't turn back to answer.

These boots were made for walking well,
Through Heaven's gates and into Hell.
I have a pair that I can sell
The coin I want is bloody.

— "Seven-League Boots," from TROLLGATE

CHAPTER TWENTY-ONE

BOOTS

We raced outside, and—once we were in the open air—the torch Magog was carrying went out for good.

The lob galloped out a moment later, carrying a canvas bag with a picture of Rhymer's Bridge embossed on the side. The bag was so heavy, he struggled with it, dragging it as he ran.

"Hey—that's the bag I was kidnapped in!" cried Magog.

"Nyaaaah," the lob said, and began a funny hoppity dance, spinning on his little goat feet. Around and around he went, till I got dizzy just watching. Then, as quickly as he'd begun his spinning, he stopped and held out the bag to me.

I took it from him.

"Nyaaaah," he cried again. Then he leaped away, over a hillock of heather, his little shaggy tail bobbing a good-bye.

Windling circled my head, twittering.

"I can't understand a word you're saying," I told her. "Slow down. Please."

Beating her wings more slowly, she hovered in front of me and sang out:

> *Some endings*
> *Are beginnings,*
> *Some failures*
> *Are winnings.*

Then, like a shooting star, she flashed away over the brow of a different hill.

Above us the moon shone full and white, making the landscape as bright as day.

"Guess we're not going to get to hear the band now," Magog said. "They were starting at moonrise. And we must be miles from home. I'm sorry, Gog. If you hadn't come after me..."

I nodded. "Then you and Windling and the shaggy lob—and the powers alone know how many others—would have been eaten by the White Wyrm. What's a band compared to that!"

Magog put his hand in mine. "You know," he said, looking up at me through the one good lens of his glasses, "there may be something in that bag to bind up your shoulder."

My shoulder! At the mention of it, it began hurting again.

A lot.

"Maybe there's something in that bag to keep us warm," I added. It was going to be cold in the woods in the middle of the night. "Pook, too."

Magog looked down. His hand went to his mouth. "I'd forgotten about Pook."

I thought, *Maybe geniuses don't always remember everything.*

"Well," I said, "Pook never forgot about you." And then, to rub it in, I added, "That's what got him into trouble in the first place."

I dumped the bag upside down to see what we had to work with.

Evidently, while Magog and I had been opening the door, the lob had been gathering up as much of Wyrm's treasure as he could. Bits of the silken cocoon and the Huntsman's boots were there as well.

"We can use that," Magog said, ripping apart some of the cocoon bits with the knife—touching only the knife's wooden handle, of course—and making a bandage. Then he unspun some of the silk and used it to tie the bandage onto my shoulder, around my arm, and then down across my chest.

Then we picked through the rest of the stuff. There

were jewels for Mom, the knife for Dad, silver and gold coins I put in my pocket.

"For some CDs," I said.

There was a strange wood-and-wire device that Magog claimed for himself, and as I had no use for it, I let him take it.

As for the boots...

"We can give those to Pook," I said, remembering them sticking out of the White Wyrm's mouth. Nothing would make me put them on myself. "He won't care."

We both shivered.

I pulled the map from the front of my trews. It was all crumpled up. A piece flaked off and fell to the ground as I unrolled it. I hoped the piece wasn't anything important.

"We're here." I showed Magog, pointing to the map. "And Pook is there." I put my finger on the brown column.

"Then let's go," Magog said. "He needs us." He gave me an enormous grin.

We headed south, and in less than an hour, we'd found the hollow tree trunk.

Pook was sitting up on top of it, legs crossed and looking crosser.

"It took you two long enough," he said. "My arm's killing me."

"How did you even know I'd gotten to Magog—"

"A fairy told me. The one on the milk carton. White-gold hair. Big blue eyes. The Weed King's granddaughter."

My jaw must have dropped.

"Really?" said Magog. He clapped his hands. "A princess. And we didn't know. She didn't seem like a princess. Did you know Windling was a princess, Gog? Did ya? Did ya?"

I swatted him, not even caring that he'd probably tell Mom. Anything to shut him up. Little brothers can be such a pain sometimes.

"No wonder the Weed King gave me the map," I said slowly. *Troll. Terribly. Thick.* "I thought he was just a lonely old man who liked company. I didn't know he was hiring me to do his dirty work." *I should have guessed, though, once I heard Windling's bad rhymes.* Only I wasn't thinking about Weed Kings then. I was thinking about...

Pook stood. "Well, she was here over an hour ago. Said you were right behind her."

"I may be a troll," I said, plain old anger getting hold of me, "but even *I* know I don't have fairy wings, Pook. We came as quick as we could."

Pook's head cocked to one side. He looked at me with his strange smile. "But you *do* have the boots," he said.

"Boots?"

How did he know?

Why should he care?

"The seven-league boots."

Magog's jaw dropped. Mine, too.

"So that's how the Huntsman got back so fast with the lob," I said aloud. "How he left me so far behind. I should have known."

Pook's lips might have been saying, *Troll. Terribly. Thick.* But I couldn't tell. He'd morphed back into a dog and I can't read dog lips real well.

Magog began jumping up and down and clapping. "Put them on, Gog. Put them on!"

I forced myself to forget how the boots looked when they were sticking out of Wyrm's mouth, how they looked dropping from the cocoon. Shaking each boot carefully, just in case there was some part of the Huntsman left in them, I pulled them on.

They fit perfectly.

Of course.

Then I stood, tied Pook to my back with some of the silk, tucked Magog and the canvas bag under my arm, and took one big seven-league step, past trees and paths and meadows and a river, and...another.

With the third step I was at the edge of the forest.

"We're almost home!" I said.

The map down the front of my trews suddenly began to get warm.

Then hot.

Then—

"Oh no!" I cried. "I almost forgot. The woodwife

warned me that I had to throw the map back or it would turn into fire."

I dropped Magog and the bag. Then I grabbed up the map and tossed it behind me, where it turned into a moth with flame red wings that flapped away into the gloom.

"That was close," Pook whispered in my ear.

"Come on," I said, picking up Magog and the bag. "A couple more steps and we're home."

I have weathered all the gales,
I have found the hidden dales,
I have told forbidden tales
To make my way back home to you.

— "I Have Walked," from BRIDGE BOUND

CHAPTER TWENTY-TWO

THE BAND

I took another step and was halfway to the next when I realized that we couldn't go home.

Not yet.

Because, in my slow troll way, I'd finally figured out that there were still too many loose ends. Which I told Magog and Pook.

So I turned a hard right instead of an easy left, and we suddenly found ourselves in front of the makeshift gate on the hill above Rhymer's Bridge.

The band was out on the floating platform, singing "I Have Walked," from *Bridge Bound,* which seemed eerily appropriate.

"Wow!" said Pook.

"We're here to finish this off," I said. "Not to listen to the band."

"No reason why we can't do both," Pook said, grinning.

I set Magog down and untied Pook from my back. Reaching into my pocket, I pulled out three of the silver coins the lob had saved from the floor of the cave and handed them to the ticket seller, a crusty-looking bodach with shaggy black hair.

"It's near the end, kids," he said. "Save your coins and buy the CD."

"I've got both CDs already," I said. "We want to go in. We've walked a long way to get here."

"Five thousand ells," said Pook.

"Five thousand hells," added Magog, and blushed at the swear.

The bodach took in my bandaged shoulder and Pook's bandaged arm, threw his head back, and laughed uproariously. "All right, then, boys, but as it's so late, I'll let you keep your coins. Only, don't tell anyone the bodach's getting soft. Ruin my reputation as a Fright, it will." He pointed at the gate. "Go on!"

I took off the seven-league boots and carried them under my unbound arm. No use taking a step and finding myself across the river and out of the Kingdom without meaning to.

Then we walked down the hill, past clumps of piskies and kelpies dancing on the grass, through knots of knockers and boggarts swaying to the tune, around troops of trows and spriggans clapping madly, by knobs of bogeys in a music trance.

"What are we looking for?" Pook asked, cradling his broken arm.

"The bad guys," I said.

"The bad guy was beaten and eaten," Magog pointed out. "And I want to hear the band. Even if it's only one song."

"Who grabbed you, little genius brother?" I asked quietly. "Who even knew you were there? The Huntsman wasn't in this alone. Remember when he said something about—"

"About his *people*?" Magog suddenly remembered.

"Yup!" I made a face. "The Huntsman never left the woods. He never grabbed you from the holdspell. Pook's nose knew."

"Hey—you're right!" said Pook, his eyebrows raised.

I wish he hadn't sounded so surprised.

We were almost to the front row, where the Queen of the sidhe and her consorts were singing along with the band.

Boots had just reached that point in the song where he sort of yodels, and the others had gathered behind him to harmonize. I felt myself beginning to hum, but only under my breath. Not all trolls can sing on key.

Very few of them, in fact.

Probably Boots, Armstrong, Cal, Iggy, and Booger

are the only trolls in the entire Kingdom who can sing on key, which is why they're so famous.

About fifteen feet in front of me, at the sound-board, the little pan was working away, his clever fingers shifting the switches, pushing them up, pushing them down, melding the strands to make the perfect sound.

Next to him was a greenkid in a tour T-shirt and camo trews, half leaning on the board, with that cool I-don't-have-a-care look.

They were both watching the stage, of course.

But I was watching them.

Who, I thought slowly, *but the pan could have even guessed we weren't full-grown trolls?*

Who, I thought, *but the pan even saw Magog asleep under the holdspell?*

Who, I thought, *but the pan would have lost a tuning device in the canvas bag?* Because I suddenly realized what the wood-and-wire thing was that Magog had kept for himself.

And who but the greenkid could have taken the bag to the wood's edge, where the Huntsman waited in his stolen seven-league boots?

That was a lot of thinking for a Troll. Terribly. Thick.

"Hey," I whispered to Magog, handing him the boots, "I have a job for you."

"For me?" His shiny face looked up at me.

"Get down to the riverbank and wade in," I said.

"Go right to the raft and give the seven-leaguers to Boots. Tell him we'll explain after the last song. Tell him to meet us at the soundboard."

"Me?" Magog said. "I can't walk the river spate by myself. I'm too young."

"Might be fear that caused it to grow," I told him, "but your hair's starting to come in. Your voice is sounding deeper. Which means it's time for you to go off on your own."

He reached up and felt the top of his head.

Grinned.

Then looked scared again.

"On your own," I said sternly. "Like you were in the cave."

His lower lip began to tremble. He wasn't quite ready.

"Do it and...and you can have my magic cards," I said.

"Really? Gosh, Gog, you *are* the greatest brother in the world." He clutched the boots to his chest.

For a moment I was embarrassed. I hadn't exactly told a lie. Trolls can't lie. But some of Pook's tricksy nature must have rubbed off on me. I knew—even if Magog didn't—that the magic cards didn't actually work. But if the promise got him going...

"Maybe not the *greatest*," I mumbled, pointing him away from the soundboard.

"Wait a minute," Pook said to Magog. "Come here."

Using his good arm, Pook cast a small glamour over Magog and—in an instant—the kid looked a little like the soundboard pan. Enough anyway. A full moon always helps magic.

Trotting off down the embankment, Magog muscled his way past the front rows and splashed into the water. Before anyone could fully pierce the glamour that disguised him—and because he looked like the soundman—no one bothered him. He made it all the way to the raft-stage, where the band was just finishing up "I Have Walked" on that last lovely lingering note.

I smiled as Boots leaned over and took the seven-leaguers.

Magog pushed back through the water, struggling a bit but never giving up. Of course, as soon as he got to the bank the small glamour had been washed away, and the Queen's Men picked him up. They threw him out, over the fence, with a stern warning.

I'd get to him in a minute.

Meanwhile the applause was deafening and the band went right into its first encore, "Trade." Then they segued into a second song, their old familiar anthem, "Meet Me."

While they sang, Boots slipped off his size twenties and put on the seven-leaguers.

As the final notes were ringing out and the rest of

the band were making their bows, Boots took one step off the stage into the water, was under Rhymer's Bridge—and a league gone.

For a moment the crowd was stunned into silence.

Then everyone stood and screamed for more.

But there was to be no more, because Boots didn't return to the stage. Instead, he must have taken a quick turn all those leagues away, because suddenly he was behind the crowd, right by the real pan, where he got out of the boots and placed them on top of the soundboard.

"What's going on here?" he asked.

The pan looked up. "Nice show, Boots," he said, but his voice betrayed his nervousness.

We'd moved quietly behind the pan.

Then Boots saw me with my bandaged shoulder, and Pook with his bandaged arm.

For a moment I trembled. My dad is a big troll, but Boots is even bigger. Close up, he's enormous. He was staring at me with eyes that were just a shade lighter than red.

"That was my little brother," I said quickly, "who gave you the boots. Only with pookah glamour, he looked like your pan."

"Where did you get them?" Boots asked, gesturing to the seven-leaguers.

I told him the short version.

And then—while he put his great hands on the pan and the greenkid so they couldn't run off—I told him the long version.

Boots yelled for the band, the Queen's Men, the Queen, and Jesse Feldman, in that order. All the while he was bellowing, "Kidnapping? Murder? Stealing from the museum? Selling drugs and silk? Using my band as a cover? My *band*?" His face and eyes turned bright red as rage surged through him. "Pieter, I will kill you."

And knowing the pan's true name, Boots could have done that without half trying.

The pan's mouth twisted in scorn. "You needed money to begin the band. I needed money to help you. As long as you didn't think to ask where the money came from, why should I have enlightened you— Troll. Terribly. Thick."

Boots's face turned redder.

His eyes went scarlet.

Cal and Iggy suddenly appeared by his side. They put their hands on his shoulders.

"Count to ten," they whispered into his ears.

Armstrong nodded.

Booger just looked bored.

Boots counted. He had to go all the way to fifty before his surge finally flowed away.

Jesse Feldman had a surge of her own, which I hadn't known was possible for a human. She drew her hand back and slapped the pan so hard, his face wore the print of her five fingers like a brand.

"If I've warned you once, pan, I've warned you a dozen times. My bands stay clean. My road crew, too. I only kept you on for Boots's sake, since you were such good friends. But no more. No more. You're fired."

The pan said nothing, but his eyes were suddenly like little brown stones.

Then the Queen, in a voice of thorns, cried out to her Men, "Arrest them! Arrest them all!"

With a flash of their wands, the Queen's Men rounded up the band, the pan, the roadies, the green-kid, Pook, Magog (from beyond the fence), and me. We were bound about with magic stronger than the Great White Wyrm's cocoon silks and compelled right then and there to tell the whole truth, which is not hard for trolls but more difficult for the magic-makers. And almost impossible for a pan.

We kids were let go immediately, of course. But the pan, the greenkid, and anyone who'd helped them got taken off to the Doom Room for proper questioning.

The Queen popped Pook to his house and sent Magog and me home hand in hand. A Queen's Man came along with us to explain things to Mom and Dad, which helped a lot. Especially after he ate a healthy bowlful of Mom's amaranth stew.

Magog kept telling everyone what a great brother I was.

They all believed him.

And, after a while, I believed him, too.

At the trial, the pan—with the red print of Jesse Feldman's fingers still on his face—tried to weasel out of trouble. Pans always do.

The greenkid just shrugged and bargained, trading for a lesser sentence by telling all he knew.

The pan got life in a human jail. We have no jails in the Kingdom. Things are simpler here—life or death.

The greenkid got ten years in another human jail. A life sentence for his kind, who need the woods and hills and valleys of the Kingdom to sustain them.

I got seats for the next year's concert for me, Magog, Pook, and anyone else I wanted to bring.

Oh—and CDs and posters autographed by the entire band.

Best of all, the band came back the next month to play at the museum—a special unplugged concert celebrating the return of the seven-leaguers.

Boots sang a song I had written the lyrics for, a song I called "Hero":

> *Strength ten,*
> *Brains zero—*
> *Funny way*
> *To be a hero.*
> *Brains zero,*

Strength ten—
Calm yourself
And count again.

Think first,
Hope fast.
Luck is best
When it can last.
Strength ten,
Brains zero—
What a way
What a way
What a way
To be a hero.

They sang it twice through, the first time with instruments and the second time a cappella, which means without accompaniment.

Boots grinned throughout the song. Armstrong snarled the words, one hand on her silent bodhran. Cal and Iggy harmonized beautifully. And Booger sang a wordless, deep *boom-boom-boom,* like a bass drum.

It was snarly all right. Gnarly, too.

Magog and Pook and I, plus our parents, all got to sit in the front row, right next to the Queen.

She said she was proud to be sitting with heroes.

Turns out she's a cousin of sorts. Many many many times removed, of course.

But then—who's counting?

A TRAVELER'S GUIDE
TO THE KINGDOM

You will have a much better and safer visit to the Kingdom of the Fey (or as they call themselves, the Folk) if you learn about the inhabitants before going there, and follow these few simple rules:

First, understand that the Kingdom is like a pyramid. The Queen and her court are at the top. Next come the magic-makers and shape-changers, like the pookahs, the fairies, and the elves. Tradesmen and workers (what we would call the middle class) are right behind them: trolls, dwarfs, pixies, brownies. The dwellers in the New Forest and the Forbidden Fields are hardly civilized and very dangerous. It is advised that you do not go where they may be found.

But *do* visit the Kingdom's museum. That's where many of the more famous artifacts of the Kingdom are stored: Queen Mab's wand, a bag of original Faerie dust, a selchie's skin, the Faery flag, the cape of Manannan MacLir, the drinking horn of Bran the Blessed, a pair of seven-league boots, a variety of silver bells that have adorned the Queen's horses, the grass green skirt of the Auld Queen, a typical pwca candle, etc.

Trade is more common in the Kingdom than coins. But some Folk will take money, as long as it is copper, silver, or gold. They have no use for tin or paper money.

Do not bring anything made of iron into the Kingdom. For most of the Fey, iron is quite painful. For some, it is downright harmful. For a few, it can kill.

Never trade with a greenman. Or a greenkid. You are sure to get the worst of the bargain.

Trolls are good workmen. Just don't make them angry.

Pookahs are a bit tricksy. Though you'll find them charming, you must not rely on them.

Pans have tongues as sharp as knives. They can cut you with a word. Don't cross them.

⬯⬯Brownies are not terribly smart. No, brownies are actually incredibly *stupid*. Don't ever ask a brownie for directions. Or for help. Or for anything.

⬯⬯Don't expect to keep secrets. Sneeze at one end of the Kingdom and the flowers will gossip about you all the way to the doctor's.

⬯⬯Remember that the Law of Harmonious Balance applies throughout the land. This means no picking flowers, no pocketing rocks, no leaving litter. Or it could—quite literally—come back to haunt you.

⬯⬯Magic comes in threes. Expect it.

⬯⬯Have a good time—a trip to the King dom can change your life if you let it.